"He can't come here. He can't know about Magnolia."

Thomas took Vi's hands in his. "So he won't."

She wished she could believe his certainty. But she'd once been certain, believed all it would take was going to the police to save her from Eric.

She'd been so wrong. "Thomas, I have to leave. I have to run. If he comes here..."

"You will be protected."

"I don't think you understand. I tried to tell people, to get help. But his entire precinct believed him. He was this close to having me committed. If I hadn't run away, he would have made it happen."

Or maybe he would have killed me. She knew how possible it was.

"This is Bent County. He doesn't control us."

"But he controls the cops and you're a cop." She hated the words the second they were out her mouth. "I'm sorry. I know you don't deserve that."

"No, I suppose I don't. But you didn't deserve what happened to you. Life isn't fair. We know that."

VANISHING POINT

NICOLE HELM

INTRIGUE

For the good ones.

Harlequin®
INTRIGUE™

ISBN-13: 978-1-335-69006-7

Vanishing Point

Copyright © 2025 by Nicole Helm

Recycling programs for this product may not exist in your area.

Harlequin Enterprises ULC
22 Adelaide St. West, 41st Floor
Toronto, Ontario M5H 4E3, Canada
www.Harlequin.com

Printed in Lithuania

MIX
Paper | Supporting responsible forestry
FSC® C021394

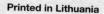

Nicole Helm grew up with her nose in a book and the dream of one day becoming a writer. Luckily, after a few failed career choices, she gets to follow that dream—writing down-to-earth contemporary romance and romantic suspense. From farmers to cowboys, Midwest to *the* West, Nicole writes stories about people finding themselves and finding love in the process. She lives in Missouri with her husband and two sons, and dreams of someday owning a barn.

Books by Nicole Helm

Harlequin Intrigue

Bent County Protectors

Vanishing Point

Hudson Sibling Solutions

Cold Case Kidnapping
Cold Case Identity
Cold Case Investigation
Cold Case Scandal
Cold Case Protection
Cold Case Discovery
Cold Case Murder Mystery

Covert Cowboy Soldiers

The Lost Hart Triplet
Small Town Vanishing
One Night Standoff
Shot in the Dark
Casing the Copycat
Clandestine Baby

Visit the Author Profile page at Harlequin.com.

CAST OF CHARACTERS

Thomas Hart—A detective with the Bent County Sheriff's Department who is surprised to find his high school sweetheart and first love back in Wyoming.

Vi Reynolds—Thomas's high school sweetheart, who moved out of Wyoming after high school graduation. Back in Bent after escaping her abusive ex.

Magnolia "Mags" Reynolds—Vi's one-year-old daughter.

Rosalie Young—Vi's second cousin. A private investigator. Lives on the Young Ranch.

Audra Young—Vi's second cousin. A rancher. Lives on the Young Ranch.

Franny Perkins—Audra and Rosalie's cousin. A writer. Lives on the Young Ranch.

Laurel Delaney-Carson—A detective with the Bent County Sheriff's Department. Thomas's good friend and mentor.

Copeland Beckett—A newer detective with the Bent County Sheriff's Department.

Eric Carter—Vi's abusive ex-husband.

Postal Inspector Dianne Kay—A postal inspector from Texas investigating mail fraud that may connect to Eric Carter.

Chapter One

Detective Thomas Hart was exhausted, and the last thing he wanted to do was go to a child's birthday party.

But he'd promised. And maybe the fun and innocence of a birthday party could wash the gross feeling of the case he'd worked today off him. He was *sure* Allen Scott had killed his wife, but so far the evidence was minimal. If he didn't drum up something soon, they were going to rule the death a suicide.

Thomas shook it off, or tried, as he pulled to a stop in front of the Delaney-Carson house out by the Delaney Ranch outside of the Bent city limits. The party was clearly already in full swing.

Years ago when his dad had gotten transferred to Arizona, his parents had wanted him to move with them. There were police jobs in Arizona, and he'd been young and unencumbered. Why not try something new, somewhere where the population didn't skew old and rancher?

But he'd liked working at Bent County. He just hadn't been able to fathom leaving. Sometimes home was just home, no matter who was around.

So, when his parents had left, he'd stayed. In the early days, he'd been a little lonely. For a variety of reasons. But these days, he had more friends that were basically family clamoring at him than he knew what to do with. He felt like he was *always* on the hook for a party. Birthdays, christenings, holidays. A never-ending onslaught.

Some he could weasel his way out of, but not this one.

Sunny Delaney-Carson was his goddaughter.

He grabbed the gift bag out of his back seat and then got out and walked up the drive. He was greeted at the door by a very skeptical seven-year-old in a sparkly blue dress, and it was somehow his life that he knew which Disney princess it correlated with.

"What is it?" she demanded, pointing at the gift bag.

Thomas held it up a little higher, because knowing Avery, she'd just shove her hand in there and yank it out. "I think the birthday girl is supposed to open it and find out."

Avery gave him a look, the kind of look he'd seen often enough from her mother. Disparaging disapproval. "She's *two*."

"And when you were *two*, you loved pulling all the paper out of the bag."

A dark-haired girl, Fern Carson-Delaney, Avery's cousin who was only a few months older than Avery herself, skittered over. She whispered in Avery's ear, then the two disappeared. No doubt to do some mischief, though Thomas never understood how Vanessa Carson and Dylan Delaney had created a child so shy.

But the world was a strange place, especially in Bent, Wyoming.

After weaving through more kids, exchanging greetings with more Delaney-Carsons and Carson-Delaneys, he finally made his way to the girl of the hour.

Sunny had Laurel's blond hair, an ability to exude as much mischief as her father, and unflagging energy at just about all times. Thomas still couldn't imagine what had possessed Laurel to have another one.

On sight, Sunny flung herself at him, so he lifted her and gave her the twirl he knew she was hoping for. She gave a squeal of delight.

"Here you go, Sunny bunny. Happy birthday."

She settled down with the gift bag, and just like her sister had a few years back, got more enjoyment out of playing with the tissue paper than finding out what was at the bottom.

"If it's a musical instrument, or anything that makes noise, I'm kicking you out," Laurel said in greeting.

"I take it that's been a theme?"

She scowled around the room. "Traitors. All of them." Then she looked at him, the scowl turning into more of a worried frown. "You look tired."

He knew she was weaseling for work information, not actually commenting on his appearance. But he pretended like he didn't know that. "I won't comment on how you look then."

She rolled her eyes. "Tough case?"

"You're on maternity leave. No police talk, remember?"

The scowl returned. "Come on. I'm getting you some food." She led him around kids and toys and all sorts of things strewn about the packed house. In the kitchen was a spread of sandwiches and chips and salads. He loaded up a plate, because Laurel would fuss otherwise, then sat down at the kitchen table and chatted casually with Laurel and her husband, Grady, who was holding their sleeping newest addition, Cary.

Thomas put in a good hour before he started to think about making his excuse to leave. A few couples with younger kids had already made their escape. But Laurel gave him the perfect out.

"You know, Thomas, I have this friend. She lives over in Fairmont. She's just so funny and—"

Thomas drained his plastic cup of the grape soda he didn't particularly like and stood. "Well, that's my cue to leave."

Laurel scowled at him. "She's nice."

"I'm sure she's great. I don't want you setting me up, Laurel."

"Why not?"

"Because you're a nosy boundary-pusher?" Grady offered lazily, Cary still asleep in the crook of his arm. He grinned at his wife.

Laurel turned the scowl on her husband, but then back to Thomas again. "You'll never find someone if you don't put yourself out there."

"Maybe I don't want to find someone."

Laurel gave him a look—much like the disdainful one her daughter had aimed at him when he'd first arrived. It made him smile. But not so much he also didn't make a break for it.

But Laurel followed. "Tell me about the case."

"No."

She groaned. "I know they gave Beckett my spot. If you're working late, it's a doozy."

"It's fine." He made it to the door.

"Is it because Beckett's a lousy detective?"

It was Thomas's turn to give her a disparaging look, though he recognized what this was *really* about. "You worried he's going to keep it when you come back?"

She smiled sweetly, but he'd seen her give that smile to enough criminals for Thomas to know it wasn't *kind*. "He can try."

Thomas laughed. "Take it easy, Laurel. Enjoy that last month."

She grumbled something, but he made it outside. Fresh air. Blessed quiet. Now he could go home and sleep. And he'd been right, all in all. All that family, those kids, birthday cake and happiness had washed some of the ugliness the case they were working on had left on him.

He drove off the Delaney-Carson property and headed home. He'd lived above the post office for years, but last year had finally sucked it up and bought a house. It was small, fit for a single guy who wasn't a spring chicken anymore. And it helped to not live over a business when he was trying to sleep off a night shift.

But it meant driving back through town, to get over to the residential area he lived in. He drove down Main, but slowed as he spotted a woman standing outside the general store, peering into the windows.

The store was closed, and the area around it was dark. He doubted she was trying to steal anything but it was hard to know for sure. He parked his car, then got out. He heard a baby crying, and realized the woman was holding a bundle.

He approached, thoughts of burglary turning into concern.

The woman turned as though she'd heard or sensed someone approach, the squalling baby in her arms. He saw the fear in her expression, so he stopped his forward movement and didn't step any closer.

He didn't recognize her, and as a lifelong resident of Bent, and a police officer in Bent County for over a decade, he knew most of the locals.

He held up one hand in a kind of surrender, used the other to pull his badge out of his pocket. "I'm a local police officer, ma'am. Can I help you with something?"

None of the fear left her face. In fact, she looked even more tense. But there was something…familiar underneath all that anxiety. He squinted, stepped a little closer without meaning to—but the light was better the closer he got.

"Vi?" He didn't mean to say it out loud, because he was certain he must be…making things up. It had been something like fifteen years since he'd seen Vi Reynolds. And maybe she'd occupied most of his growing-up years, and still that soft first-love place in his heart, but there'd be no reason for grown-up Vi to be here now.

She'd left Bent a long time ago, and she didn't have any family left nearby that he remembered. Maybe some cousins or something, but not *in* Bent, and no one she was close to. Or had been.

But…

"Thomas," she said after several quiet moments ticked by. "You… You look different."

"God, I hope so. I think I weighed a buck ten soaking wet the last time I saw you."

She laughed at that, shifted the baby onto her other hip. But that tension didn't leave her. Not fully. Maybe because the baby was still whimpering. But she didn't say anything else.

"Uh, so, are you visiting?" he prompted.

"Um." She looked back at a car parallel parked—poorly— a few yards away. It had Wyoming plates. "I moved back a little while ago. I… I'm living out closer to Sunrise. My cousins have a ranch."

Thomas nodded, not sure what to do with this very strange trip down memory lane. But her baby was crying, and she was standing outside the closed general store. "Can I help you with something?"

"I just… Mags is running a bit of a fever, and I ran out

of Tylenol. I thought the general store was open until six."
She gestured helplessly at the store.

"Not anymore. Closes at four on Sundays."

"I should have checked." She smiled thinly. "That's what
I get for thinking I know things. I guess I'll drive up to
Fairmont. Surely something there is open?" she asked, a
little desperately.

The baby was inconsolable, and Vi looked like she
wanted to melt into the concrete. Thomas glanced around.
"Yeah, you'll have a few options, but hey, just wait here
one second, okay? Just one minute."

She frowned but nodded. Reluctantly, he could admit.
Still, she nodded. So he jogged around the back of the store.
His friends Zach and Lucy were staying in the apartment
above with their two-year-old while their house out in Hope
Town was getting a new addition for *their* upcoming new
addition. Surely they'd have something on hand.

Vi Reynolds figured as far as rock bottoms went, she'd
already reached hers. So running into her ex-boyfriend
while she looked like a bedraggled sea witch and Magnolia screamed her adorable little head off wasn't going any
deeper in the rock bottom department.

It was just icing on the garbage cake of her life.

And still, this was all better than what she'd managed
to drag herself out of. She reminded herself of that, almost
every single day.

Magnolia wriggled and did that awful head swinging
thing that usually ended with them *both* crying when head
smacked into head.

"Come on, baby. I know you're miserable, but now I
am too, if it helps any." She tried to hum a lullaby as she
bounced Magnolia, who was as exhausted as she was cranky

from the fever. Vi tried to offer Mags quiet reassurances, but her throat was getting too tight. She should just get in her car and drive. What could Thomas possibly manage to do?

Thomas Hart.

God, she'd loved that skinny little goofball. He wasn't skinny anymore. No, he looked very…sturdy. And that baby face had aged. Same blue eyes, but the face had that…rugged Western look about it. Broad shoulders that had once housed a skinny frame now looked more filled out. His hair was cut short, so the color was some indistinguishable light brown, and his eyes…

Well, they were the exact same. It sent a pang of longing through her—for a simpler time, for a time before she'd made so many mistakes.

Why did he have to be *hot* now? Instead of just cute and sweet?

Well, he probably wasn't sweet anymore. He was a cop. He'd pulled out a badge. Just the thought made her tense. She knew how that went, didn't she?

She squeezed Magnolia tighter. "Let's run, Mags," she muttered. She even took a step back to turn and go, but Thomas reappeared before she could even get her keys out of her purse.

He was holding a box of children's Tylenol. He held it out to her. It was opened.

Why would he have access to children's Tylenol? Opened at that? Did he have kids? Oh, God, he probably had a parcel of them with some beautiful, skinny, smart, perfect mother who didn't run out of medicine.

He took the bottle out of the box, pulled one of the little syringes they gave out at pharmacies for oral medication for babies. He unwrapped it. "How much?" he asked, like he did this all the time.

She found herself absolutely speechless at the idea of him married with kids, which was ludicrous since she'd been married for a time. And had a child.

He smiled at her gently. "I'm friends with a ton of people with babies." He didn't ask, but she could *feel* the question in the air.

Is she yours?

Vi hugged Mags a little tighter.

"My friends live upstairs," he said. "They've got a kid, so I know how it all works. How much?"

She told him the correct dosage for Magnolia's weight. She watched him expertly fill the syringe with the right dosage, then hold it out to her. But she had both hands supporting Mags, so then he offered it to the baby.

Mags leaned forward a little and took the medicine. She'd always been a good medicine taker, probably because she'd been so sickly those first few months. But she was healthy now.

They were *both* healthy and safe. And no matter her failures, that was all that could matter.

Except in this moment, Vi's high school sweetheart was feeding her baby medicine. On a dark street in the middle of their hometown.

Vi wished she could travel back in time. For a blinding, painful moment. She'd take their breakup moment over this one, and that had been...

Awful. Gut-wrenching. Because no amount of being foolish and eighteen and desperately in love with each other had allowed their dreams for a future to match.

What would her life have been like if she'd compromised?

The question nearly took her out at the knees. She'd crumble under the weight of all those what-ifs if she gave this any more time. "Thank you. Thank your friends for me. I really have to go."

He handed the now-empty syringe and box to her. "They insisted."

She swallowed at the lump in her throat. "Thanks."

"Any time."

He stepped back. Once. Twice. "Hope I see you around, Vi." Then he turned and walked away.

She did not return the sentiment but noted he didn't drive away until she did.

Chapter Two

Thomas didn't consider himself a stick-in-the-mud. He'd learned in his years as a deputy and then a detective that, sometimes, a few rules had to be bent.

But if he looked Vi Reynolds up in the county's computer system, he definitely wasn't bending rules for the right reasons. Just to satisfy his curiosity. Which wasn't right.

But he hadn't been able to get the other night out of his head.

He knew fifteen years changed a person. Hell, he was hardly the guy he'd been at eighteen. Being a cop had changed him, hardened him in some ways, matured him in others. No doubt Vi had gone through her fair share of growing up and maturing in fifteen years.

But she'd seemed sad. Beat down. More than just because of a screaming baby. Like life had been considerably unkind.

Which shouldn't matter to him. They hadn't kept in touch. He didn't know her anymore. Hell, she had a kid and probably a husband.

But the interaction had settled inside of him, like yet another regret when it came to her.

Now she was back, or near Sunrise anyway, where she'd always claimed she didn't want to be.

He hadn't been able to leave back then—in high school he'd worked hard to complete a program to go to community college for free. He'd had a plan to move straight into the police academy once he turned twenty-one. He hadn't been able to afford to go anywhere else.

Vi'd had big dreams and a full ride to Clemson. Premed. Get out of small-town Wyoming. Get away from her parents' constant fighting. Build her own big, beautiful, amazing life.

He had loved her, wanted her to have all those things, but he knew he didn't fit in her plans. The end had been hard, but he'd always been pretty certain it was the right thing for both of them, no matter how hard.

Over the years, when none of his relationships had worked out, he'd always wondered what might have been different if he'd been able to find a way. Move almost across the country with nothing in his pocket, make something work.

But mostly, he felt he'd ended up right where he should, so how could he regret the choices that had led him there?

"Going to stare at that screen any longer?"

Thomas looked up from his laptop to his current partner, standing in the doorway of their shared office.

Copeland Beckett was a rare out-of-state transfer. Most Bent County deputies were homegrown, or at least from Wyoming, and that meant those in charge tended to be Bent County natives and tended to promote from within their community.

But when Laurel had gone out on maternity leave *again*, Sheriff Buckley had decided Copeland—what with his big-city experience in Denver—should take her place in the detective bureau.

Bent County was growing, and with growth came more

complicated cases. Thomas wouldn't be surprised if by the time Laurel got back, they'd have to be a three-person department.

Thomas liked Copeland well enough, though he was a bit...unpredictable. There was definitely what Thomas could only describe as big-city energy pumping off the guy. He wanted action. He wanted results.

Thomas didn't have the first clue how he'd wound up in Bent County, but Copeland wasn't one to spill about his private life, unless it was about his superficial, social one.

Thomas wasn't sure how Copeland and Laurel would get along. But that was a problem for later.

For now, he dealt with Copeland just fine, and he had indeed been staring too long at an empty search screen.

"Did you get the coroner report yet?" Thomas asked, ignoring Copeland's question.

"No."

Damn it. "Regardless of if the report is ready or not, let's see if Gracie will take a meeting with us tomorrow."

"I can give her office a call right now."

Thomas waved him away. "She's Laurel's cousin. I'll do it."

"Is Laurel related to everyone?"

Thomas might have found the disgust in Copeland's tone funny if he could find any humor in this case. Before he could pull out his phone to call Gracie, Vicky, currently working the desk, poked her head into their office.

"Rosalie Young here to see you, Hart. Want to see her or have her come back some other time?"

It wasn't unusual for a private investigator to want to talk to him. He'd had meetings with Rosalie over the years since she'd been working for Fools Gold Investigations out of Wilde, and any other PIs who worked there. Usually Rosalie scheduled them in advance, but answering questions for a PI sounded a hell of a lot better than dealing with his current predicament. "You can send her in."

Vicky nodded and left.

"I'll call Gracie. If it needs the Bent native touch, I'll let you know." Then Copeland followed Vicky out. Not five seconds later, Rosalie entered.

And seeing Rosalie Young in person made it all click. Maybe it was the red hair, maybe it was just bound to be a memory that popped back eventually.

The Young family were those cousins of Vi's who lived in the area. Rosalie and Vi hadn't been close. They weren't the same age. He *knew* they hadn't been close because he'd known Vi's life in and out, back then.

But Rosalie had an older sister. Thomas couldn't remember her name for the life of him. He still didn't think Vi had been close with her either, but it was possible he didn't remember *everything* from fifteen years ago.

Besides, Rosalie did indeed live out by Sunrise, on a ranch with her sister. Which sounded a lot like what Vi had said the other night.

"Vi mentioned she ran into you the other night," Rosalie said, making herself at home in his office as she so often did. Quinn Peterson, the head of Fools Gold, tended to hire women like her. Brash, unafraid, and tough as nails.

"I didn't realize…" He didn't often find himself completely speechless these days. He'd been through a hell of a lot. But he really had no idea how to deal with this situation. "I guess I forgot there was a connection."

Rosalie smiled thinly, but she didn't say anything to that, which wasn't like her. Usually she said whatever the hell she wanted.

"We've got a little issue out at the ranch. Vi's…a little

uncomfortable with cops. I've been trying to get her to let us bring in some help, but I didn't know you two…knew each other. Until she mentioned it. I think she'd trust you. Anyway, can you come out to the ranch tonight? I know it's a drive, but…"

"Somebody in trouble?"

"*I* think so."

"Vi?"

Rosalie popped right back to her feet. She never did sit still long. "Just come on out, huh? Audra will make a cake or some cookies or something. She's a hell of a baker."

Right. *Audra* was the older sister's name. He didn't think Vi and Audra had been close, but maybe he just didn't remember. Didn't really matter. "If someone's in trouble, you don't have to bribe me with cake, Rosalie. I'm an officer of the law."

She studied him for a second, then smiled a little. But she definitely wasn't herself. "You're a good guy, Hart. We're gonna need one of those."

Vi FELT ALMOST human again. Magnolia's congestion was finally starting to clear up and she was sleeping better, so Vi was too. She'd even gotten a shower with Magnolia down for the night. And now that she was clean and Mags was sleeping, Vi could actually go downstairs and eat dinner with everyone.

She didn't know what she would have done without her second cousins. It had been a crazy, last-ditch effort to call them up out of the blue last year—people she'd only seen at funerals and family get-togethers even when she'd still lived in Wyoming.

And they'd taken her in, very few questions asked. They'd given her not just a home, but a place first to hide, then to heal, and finally to bring her baby home to. They'd kept her going through Mags's stint in the NICU, and when they'd finally brought Magnolia home, they—along with their fourth roommate, Rosalie and Audra's cousin on their mom's side—had fed her, taken turns with nighttime feedings, ensured that not only Magnolia thrived, but Vi did too.

They'd become her best friends in the world, her family, her support.

The other night had been the first time in months she'd felt overwhelmed, and that was only because Franny had been away on her book tour, Audra had been at some women-in-agriculture meeting, and Rosalie had been off on a case.

Vi didn't let herself get self-recriminatory about not being able to handle it all on her own. The old Vi would have blamed herself, called herself every terrible name in the book, and known she was an utter failure as a person and mother.

But new Vi—the woman who was going to be strong for her baby girl and find a *life* after the horrible things she'd been through—had accepted that everyone, especially mothers, had bad nights when their babies were sick.

Maybe they didn't *all* run into their hotter-than-they-were-in-high-school ex-boyfriends when that happened, but...

She paused on her way down to the dining room, as she had multiple times over the past few days when Thomas had popped into her mind.

It was so strange. She didn't trust cops. She'd made that mistake in so many blinding colors, and had vowed to never, *ever* let herself fall into that trap again.

But this was *Thomas*. It was hard to imagine him as a cop, as a detective, even though that had always been his plan. He'd been one of the sweetest guys she'd ever known, and that was a direct contrast with the police officers she'd had dealings with over the past few years.

Well, she supposed she could have a fun little fantasy where he was that hot, *not* a cop, and she was anywhere near capable of rekindling some old high school flame. Because it was only ever going to be a *fantasy*.

She shook her head, started heading for the dining room again. The doorbell rang almost at the same time she was about to pass the front door.

"I'll get it," Vi called out. She hated answering the door still, which was ridiculous. In the almost two years since she'd finally left him, Eric had never once tried to come here. Sure, he still left her threatening messages sometimes—no matter how many times she changed her phone number—same with emails and the like, but he wasn't going to expend any energy to come all the way from Richmond to *nowhere* Wyoming.

He'd have done that by now if he wanted to, she was sure of it.

Had to believe it.

"No, I will!" Rosalie shouted from deeper in the house. She came barreling out of the kitchen like a wild woman, which was not *unlike* her younger cousin.

"Hey, thought you were showering," Rosalie said, sliding to a stop in front of Vi like she was going to jump between her and the door.

Which was a bit much, even for the energetic Rosalie.

Vi pointed at her wet hair. "Yeah, I was."

"You know, you've had a rough week. Why don't you head back upstairs and I'll bring dinner up to you?"

"No, I'd like some company. I'd like to feel like a normal human being."

Rosalie opened her mouth, but no words came out. She looked like she was scrambling for some other excuse. Which made no sense.

Vi pointed at the door. "Are you going to open the door?"

"Oh, it's probably some salesman."

"Rosalie, no salesman is coming all the way out here in the middle of nowhere. What is going on?"

"Nothing! *Nothing.* Was that Mags? I thought I heard a cry."

Vi pointed to the baby monitor hooked to her waistband. Then went ahead and moved past Rosalie and twisted the doorknob open.

"Vi—"

But if she mounted any other excuse, Vi didn't hear it. Because there on the porch stood Thomas Hart. He was dressed much as he had been the other night. Slacks. A sort of business casual polo shirt underneath an unzipped jacket.

Everything kind of stopped for a second. "Thomas." She didn't know how he did it. Looked so completely like the boy she remembered, and yet so much...well, *better.* *Men.* They had all the luck.

He smiled. Kindly. But she recognized that type of kind. It was saved for victims.

Vi turned to look at Rosalie. Shock and betrayal stung deep. She'd done this. She'd...*told* him. "Why did you do this?"

Rosalie got that stubborn look about her, dark blue eyes flashing. "Because I wanted someone's professional opinion."

"It's not yours to want a professional opinion on," Vi said through gritted teeth. She turned to Thomas, trying to smile. "She shouldn't have brought you all the way out here."

He looked completed unfazed by any of this. He shrugged. "I don't mind."

"Surely whoever you go home to minds."

"Not going home to anyone these days."

He said that without breaking eye contact, with that same, easy forthrightness he'd always had. And she blushed in spite of herself, because that had sounded like fishing.

Because it was. Even though it shouldn't be and she hadn't really *meant* to fish. "I... I didn't mean it like that."

His smile was still kind, but a little...something else. Not pitying, she knew that, because it made her heart do all those old flippy things it used to.

"I know."

Rosalie cleared her throat. Right. Vi was *furious*, and not talking to Thomas Hart about *anything*.

"I don't know why Rosalie has overstepped like this, but I can assure you, everything is fine."

"Have him listen to the voicemail and we'll see if he thinks it's fine."

Vi glared at Rosalie. "It's nothing," she said through gritted teeth again, trying to send Rosalie a million warning glares.

Rosalie took none of them. She crossed her arms over her chest, looking even more stubborn. "It's not nothing." She turned to Thomas. "He keeps leaving her threatening voicemails."

"Who is he?" Thomas asked, still standing on the porch like he dealt with this kind of thing all the time.

Because he's a cop. "No one," Vi said bitterly. "Now, you can go—" She was trying to edge Rosalie out of the way, close the door on Thomas as nicely as she could, but Rosalie reached out a hand and stopped the door's forward movement.

"Her ex-husband. His name is—"

Vi felt as though the blood just…rushed out of her head. Tears threatened so fast, she didn't know how to stop them. She had worked so hard to feel in control, to get her *life* back.

Rosalie was *ruining it.* "How dare you," she managed.

"I am worried about your safety, Vi. I don't understand why you won't take this seriously."

"Seriously? Seriously? I got out. I got divorced. I *left.*"

"He's still harassing you."

"I tried to stop him. I *tried.* And he very nearly had me committed. So I left. I ran away. I *stay* away because there's no beating him. He wants to poke at me, what do I care? As long as he stays most of a country away, *I* don't care. I'm not risking Magnolia to try to beat him."

"What about stopping him?" Rosalie demanded.

"There is no stopping him. There never will be." She looked from Rosalie to Thomas, embarrassment swamping her. She could not stand here and do this. She just *couldn't.* She'd said her piece. "If you'll excuse me, I have to check on my daughter." Then she turned away from both of them and stormed upstairs.

She wasn't hungry anymore.

Chapter Three

"I thought that would go better," Rosalie said with a scowl.

"I'm not sure why you did," Thomas replied. "Don't you help investigate things for women who've…" He wanted to choose his words carefully. Both for Rosalie's sake, and because he didn't like the idea of using any reckless words on Vi. "Been through it? You should understand how little a victim likes being treated like a child."

"I wasn't treating her like a child."

"You called a cop behind her back and against her will. And clearly gave her no warning after inviting me here."

"If I gave her warning, she wouldn't have *been* here."

"It doesn't seem like her being here worked out."

"I want you to listen to the voicemail," Rosalie said, clearly undeterred.

"No." God, he wanted to. He wanted to sweep in and immediately fix this for Vi. Whatever it was. But she'd looked absolutely…betrayed by Rosalie.

He couldn't add to it. What was more, he knew that in cases like this—whatever the details might be—if the victim didn't want help, there wasn't much he could do about it.

"Hart."

"If she wants my take, she'll bring it to me. Otherwise, you need to let this lie."

"And if it escalates?"

He didn't have a quick and easy answer for that. Because he wanted details. Names. And it wasn't *just* because he'd been in love with Vi a million years ago. He dealt with too many victims of harassment, abuse. He'd seen too many men get away with it.

He was currently in the midst of a case where someone was getting away with it.

He wanted any man that small and vicious to pay.

But it wasn't up to him. "You're licensed to carry a gun, and I know you've got plenty. Didn't Audra win some sharpshooting contest not that long ago?"

Rosalie sighed. "We might be tough as nails, Hart, and I know you probably can't understand this because men are so predictable, but being able to defend yourself doesn't mean you'll have the opportunity to."

He thought of every case he'd failed to solve, every call he'd been able to do *jack shit* in time to stop something terrible from happening. "Pretty well-versed in that, actually, Rosalie."

Rosalie looked at him, pleading in her eyes instead of frustration. "Can't you try to get through to her?"

She was clearly changing tactics. It was beyond obvious. Unfortunately, Thomas was not immune to obvious. "I know you're worried, but—"

"You don't have to change her mind," Rosalie said quickly. "Just…talk to her from like a police perspective, but also like a guy she knows."

"We don't know each other, Rosalie. Not really. High school was a long time ago."

"But you're the best shot we have of her actually listening to someone. You know as well as I do that burying your head in the sand of a problem asshole doesn't make the asshole disappear."

Which was more true than he liked to acknowledge. It wasn't like his job allowed him a *ton* of faith in humanity, but he tried to maintain some.

And that was how he found himself going up the stairs, and then knocking on the last door on the right, per Rosalie's instructions.

"Rosalie, you need to give me some space," the voice on the other side of the door said.

"It's Thomas."

A long pause. Maybe she wouldn't open the door, but he waited.

Eventually the knob turned.

She opened the door but stood in the doorway clearly not wanting to talk to him, clearly not wanting him to have a glimpse inside.

"She had no right to call you," she said firmly.

"No, she didn't."

Vi let out a sigh, but she said nothing else. He supposed she didn't look *exactly* the same as she had in high school, but she was just as pretty as she'd been back then. Even with her deep auburn hair wet and her dark blue eyes full of sadness. He'd once had that little pattern of freckles across her nose memorized.

He kept thinking this *ache* around his heart would ease, what with the passage of fifteen years, but it seemed to only twist. But the past—*their* past—wasn't why he was here.

"I don't want to get in between anything going on with your family," Thomas said, choosing his words carefully. Or trying to. "I certainly don't… Hell, Vi, I might feel like I know you because of high school, but I know people change a hell of a lot from eighteen to thirty-three. We're practically strangers. I don't expect you to just…believe I'm the same guy I was. Or trust me with something like this. I didn't come up here to change your mind about anything."

"Then why did you come up here?" she asked skeptically.

"To tell you that I believe in helping people. I always have, and I *always* will. No matter how often that's been an incredibly complicated thing. I don't expect you to want my help. I just want to make it clear. You can trust me, and I will help in whatever ways I can. Whenever and however that happens." He held out his business card to her.

She looked at it, clearly not about to take it.

"You never have to use it if you don't want to. What's the harm in just having it?"

He could see her relenting, but she still didn't take it from him.

So he tried to lighten the mood a little. "And you don't have to use it for professional reasons."

She frowned at him, but he saw a little spark of humor in her eyes, as he'd hoped.

"Are you flirting with me?"

"Sure. Why not?"

"I'm a single mother with a terrible ex-husband and tons of baggage, and I certainly don't look like I did when I was eighteen."

Maybe not. But the impact of her hadn't changed, even if she had. "You look just fine to me."

She shook her head, but her mouth had curved ever so slightly. "You always were a sweet-talker."

"Lots of things change, but not everything."

"Thomas."

"Just take it, Vi." And when she finally did, he considered that a win for the day. He knew when to retreat. He stepped back. "Hopefully I'll see you around." Then he turned and left.

And was *slightly* gratified that he didn't hear her door close until he was halfway down the stairs.

Vi REALLY WANTED to stay in her room and pout and sulk, but she was hungry. And, weirdly, Thomas had taken away *some* of that cloud of embarrassment and shame. He'd made her smile, just a little bit.

Just like always.

But of course they'd changed. God, she wasn't sure she'd even recognize eighteen-year-old Vi. So sure she'd become a doctor and conquer the world.

Now she was everything she'd told Thomas she was—a divorced single mom with a ton of baggage. A *victim*.

You look just fine to me.

He was probably just saying that to be nice. Trying to cajole her into…whatever it was Rosalie was trying to make happen. She was going to have to convince herself there'd been no actual flirting.

She didn't know him anymore. He was a cop. No doubt he looked at her and saw a pitiful victim.

But he hadn't treated her like one, and the way he'd smiled at her had reminded her of all those years ago when he'd first done it and asked her to go to the homecoming dance with him in ninth grade.

It was a million years ago, but he made it seem like not *so* much time had passed. At least for a few minutes.

But time had indeed passed. A lot of time. And not just time, but an entire lifetime of mistakes on her part.

Besides, she'd been back in Bent County for almost a full year and had managed to avoid running into him or anyone else she knew by spending most of her time on the ranch. And she liked it that way. She liked the life she was building out here where it felt like no one could reach her.

She had family—not just Mags, but actual family. And it was because they'd become her family in heart as well as blood, Vi didn't stay in her room sulking.

Well, and because she was starving after all.

When she got to the dining room, Rosalie and Audra were already at the table, eating and chatting. Franny was still off on her book tour for another two days. Since Vi didn't have a job, she usually handled the household duties—like cleaning and making dinner—but since Mags had been sick everyone had insisted she take the week off.

So someone else had made dinner. Vi was determined she would at least clean up after it. She had to earn her keep *some* way.

Both sisters looked up when she entered the dining room. Audra smiled. Rosalie looked sheepish. Which was how Vi knew that Rosalie hadn't told Audra about this.

"Your sister had Thomas Hart come out here, without telling me."

"Rosalie," Audra said, clearly pained and, as ever, despairing of her sister.

"You listened to the same voicemail I did," Rosalie said, scowling. "The threats are escalating."

"I'm not going to have you listen to any of them after this," Vi returned, sitting down at the table. She didn't know what possessed her to let Rosalie listen in the first place.

"She isn't...wrong about that, Vi," Audra said, clearly concerned. "This did sound more...violent."

Vi refused to accept it, even if it was true. "He wants me to live in fear. I won't do it. I'm certainly not going to ask for help from a cop." Maybe she had a hard time believing Thomas would be like Eric, but it hadn't just been

Eric that she'd had to deal with back in Richmond. It had been his whole squad.

Every last one of them either so taken in by Eric they couldn't see the truth, or just…didn't care about the truth. Too many of them had figured it was her fault that Eric liked to knock her around.

She took a seat next to Audra and accepted the passed casserole dish.

"Thomas isn't just *any* cop. You know him. Like biblically."

Vi spared Rosalie a scolding look. "That was fifteen years ago."

"So?"

"I knew my ex-husband *biblically* too. Enough to have a child. Should I ask for his help?"

Rosalie grunted in frustration.

"I know you're worried. If you want me to leave—"

Audra put her hand over Vi's. "Don't do that," she said in her soft way. Even though Audra was tough on the outside, with her ranching and sharpshooting, and her ability to handle the rough-and-tumble life out here in the middle of nowhere, she was such a gentle softie underneath it all. "We're not worried because it's trouble, we're worried about *you*."

Which made Vi want to cry. She didn't know why her two second cousins she'd barely known growing up had taken such a risk to get involved with her life. How they were so good at pulling her into the fold, accepting her and Magnolia as family. How this had begun to feel like a real, good life instead of the nightmare she'd escaped.

She filled her plate, gave herself a second to get her emotions under control. And then she worked on letting anger and resentment go.

Because it didn't get them anywhere.

"I understand why you did it, Rosalie. And if I ever..." She had a hard time saying the words, because she had to believe it would never, ever happen. "If there's ever a real threat, where he might actually come here, I'll call Thomas. I promise."

And she prayed like hell that would never be the case.

Chapter Four

"The prosecutor isn't going for it."

Thomas didn't look up at Copeland. He knew he'd see his own frustrations and powerlessness reflected back at him. "So what now?"

"I wish I knew." Too many dead ends in the case, and Thomas knew he couldn't blame the lawyers. They needed evidence, a case. They couldn't go on his word and his gut.

But Thomas *knew* that guy had killed his wife and staged it as a suicide. There was too much history of assault there. Too many inconsistencies in how the body had been found.

And there just wasn't anything he could do, unless they found some real damning evidence somewhere along the line.

It was time to take off for the day, and he had to get over to Wilde for yet another party. Copeland walked outside with him, neither of them saying anything.

But once outside, with radios and cameras turned off and put away in their cars, Thomas and Copeland faced each other.

"I got the name of a bar he frequents over in Fairmont," Copeland said, squinting into the sunset. "Might find myself there tonight."

They couldn't both go. It was too obvious. Still, Thomas

found himself conflicted. "I've got an engagement party to go to."

"You've sure got a lot of parties to attend for a single guy."

"You try never moving out of your hometown. Look, we can't take risks here. The prosecutor is already being too careful. One wrong move, and he won't look at *anything* we find."

"I'm just going out for a drink, Hart," Copeland said with a grin. "What could possibly go wrong?"

But Thomas knew. Copeland could push too far and screw the case. Still, for all his big-city brashness, Copeland wasn't the type to botch a case. So Thomas just rolled his eyes. They parted ways, and Thomas got into his car.

The drive over to Wilde wasn't too long. And he'd just make a quick appearance. Say hi to his cousins, his friends. Congratulate Dunne and Quinn. Then he'd go home and…

What? Wallow?

No. He'd just…go over the case again. So what if it'd be the hundredth time? That was the job. Tedious going over things until you found the one thing that led you to the next thing and so on.

He wasn't giving up on this, not yet. Even if the prosecutor wouldn't take it, that didn't mean he had to stop investigating.

The party was being held out at the Thompson Ranch—a place that had once belonged to his no-good uncle, where his cousins had grown up. Amberleigh had passed away, but Zara and Hazeleigh still lived on the property with their husbands.

Cars littered the yard in front of the ranch house. Even with the cold temperatures, the front door was open. Thomas stepped inside. Chatter buzzed, people were packed into corners, and a makeshift bar was set up on the kitchen counter.

He could use a drink, he decided. Just *one* since he was driving home, but before he could greet people, wind his way through the crowd, he stopped short.

Standing there, hiding a bit in the corner, was Vi Reynolds. She was watching Rosalie, who was in the kitchen pouring shots, with a slight smile on her face. Her hair was down around her shoulders. It was dry, so it looked redder than when he'd seen her out at the Young Ranch. It looked like she had on the tiniest bit of makeup, which reminded him of the first time he'd danced with her.

Homecoming. Ninth grade. She'd smelled like strawberries and smiled at him like she had all the answers to every secret in the universe.

"Hey, you made it."

Thomas had to drag his gaze away from Vi and look at his cousin. "Hey, Zara." He chatted with Zara for a minute, then tried to move away with the excuse of going to get a drink.

But he wanted to get to Vi. Old habits and memories from fifteen years ago apparently died very hard.

As he moved for the bar, he didn't see her anymore. He frowned, scanning the room. He ended up having to congratulate Quinn and Dunne, answer Sarabeth's—a teen he'd once saved from a burning building—determined questions for a gruesome story she was writing for school.

Once he got free of people, he surveyed the room again and still didn't see Vi, but Rosalie hadn't left yet, so—

He turned, just as someone was coming in from the hallway where the bathroom was.

And then they simply stood face-to-face.

"Oh," she said on an exhale. "Hi."

Her eyes had always reminded him of those bright cold days in the middle of winter. A piercing kind of blue. And he wanted to laugh. Everything that had happened to him in his fifteen years of being a cop could fade away in that color. He could stand here, an adult man with a hell of a lot of experience under his belt, and still find himself tongue-tied over his high school girlfriend.

"Hi."

She looked away, gestured toward the kitchen. "Rosalie tricked me into coming. Her date fell through, and she said she couldn't bear celebrating love alone. But she couldn't bail on her boss's engagement party, and Audra's a big, mean stick-in-the-mud who hates parties, so I *had* to come and let Audra watch Magnolia." She gestured over to where Rosalie was taking a shot with the bride-to-be. "I think she just wanted a designated driver."

"She's a tricky one."

Vi laughed. "Yeah. I assume you know the bride or groom?"

"Both, kind of. Two of Dunne's brothers are married to my cousins. You remember Zara and Hazeleigh, right?"

"Sure. The triplets."

"Amberleigh passed away, so it's just the two of them now. With my parents in Arizona, and their mom passed, I tend to be folded into the holiday celebrations, so I've gotten to know Dunne and Quinn. Besides, I deal with Quinn and her PIs, like your cousin, at work from time to time."

"No escaping the ties in Bent County, is there?"

He wasn't sure she said that disparagingly or with a kind of wistfulness. He'd never left, so he couldn't really imagine. Maybe it was both. "You said you've been back for a while, and it's taken me this long to run into you."

"And now we've run into each other twice in two weeks."

"Must be fate."

She shook her head and rolled her eyes, but her smile didn't dim. "You don't believe in fate."

"Didn't."

"Oh really? And what changed your mind?"

He thought about the stories he could tell, about people in this room alone. The horrible things they'd seen, but *something* had brought them to the other side. A better, happier side.

But those weren't his stories to tell. Still, he had some of his own. And one even involved her, sort of.

"About eight years ago, when I was still a very young and eager deputy, two armed men stormed the station to free someone we had in holding. They were connected to the mob, on the search for their boss's kid. It was a whole thing."

"Clearly."

"Anyway, seconds before they come in and fire the first shot, I was standing at the front desk talking to someone on the phone. I hung up, and I saw something out of the corner of my eye on the ground. A little flash of silver. I wouldn't have thought anything of it, probably, but it was a dime."

He watched her face, the bolt of recognition that changed her expression from a little uncomfortable, to more invested.

"I remembered how you always said a dime was a sign from your grandfather saying hello. I didn't think any spirits were saying hello to me, but still, because of your story I bent down and picked it up. The first shot—that likely would have got me in the head—missed me." He could still remember the way the sound had exploded around them, just as his fingers had brushed the dime on the floor. "They still shot me—but in the side. It was bad, but I survived it."

"That…wasn't fate," she said but was quiet. Maybe shaken.

In fairness, it was probably too much to bring up at a party when they'd barely seen each other in fifteen years. Because it *had* been bad. The worst he'd ever been hurt, though not the first or last time. Still, he couldn't deny that he always remembered that dime.

"Felt like fate to me."

She blinked, then looked down and away. He should find something more casual to talk about. Something…about the old days or…the weather. "Can I grab you a drink? Maybe we can—"

She held up her phone. "I have to go call Audra and check in on Magnolia."

Ouch. He nodded, and even though the rejection hurt, he kept his smile in place. "Sure."

"It was…nice seeing you again," she said, clearly just trying to be polite and not meaning it *at all*. Then she smiled a little and turned to walk away.

Well, it sucked, but he figured that was that.

But he watched her go, and she looked back over her shoulder. Their eyes meeting. He knew he should keep his big mouth shut, but history was a hell of a thing.

"You know I gave you my number, but I don't have yours," he said, across the few steps she'd taken away.

He watched her hesitate. But hesitation wasn't refusal, and he'd hold on to that, even if she didn't give him her phone number.

Then she stepped back toward him, held out her hand, palm up.

He typed in his phone password, then handed it over to her. She went to Contacts and added her name and number. For a moment, she hesitated again, then looked up at him and gave him the phone back.

"I can't promise I'll answer if you call," she said, very

seriously. But that wasn't a *don't call*. She was conflicted. He could be respectful of conflicted.

"Okay, then I'll text."

He watched her try to fight a smile and lose. He felt all of fourteen again, but she nodded once before she turned away and weaved her way through the crowd.

VI HADN'T *MEANT* to start dating Thomas.

Again.

Over the next few weeks, it just seemed to…happen. He'd started with texting her, like he'd said at the party. Sometimes he'd ask if she remembered something from high school. Sometimes he'd ask if she'd seen a movie or liked some band—usually one she'd never heard of. When he asked if she wanted to go out to see a movie, she'd told him no.

He was a cop. She had sworn off cops. If there were any signs from the universe, it was that his chosen profession was one she couldn't trust or be comfortable with.

She'd changed her mind the very next day. Mostly because Audra, Rosalie and Franny wouldn't let up on it and this would shut them up.

But also because she couldn't get the story of him being *shot* out of her head. Because yes, back in the old days she'd believed in silly things like dimes and seeing 11:11 on the clock were her late grandparents saying hello.

And she wanted to find something to believe in again. Nothing about that felt safe.

Except it was Thomas Hart, and he'd *always* been her safety net. When her parents had been screaming at each other, when the divorce had gotten nasty, when her stepmother had overstepped, or one of mom's boyfriends had gotten…handsy.

Thomas had always been the safest place she could find.

So she went to a movie with him. All these years later, she'd gone on a date with her first boyfriend. And when he'd kissed her cheek before dropping her off, she had wanted so *badly* to have this kind of normal again. She didn't know who else she'd be able to have it with, because the thing about Thomas was she'd known him for *years*.

She'd loved him, hard and long. He'd been her first. They'd had their fights, disagreements and dramas, but he'd never been mean to her. He'd never hurt her. A foundation existed there.

He took her and Magnolia on a picnic on a particularly nice day. He even came to a dinner at the ranch, dealt with Franny, Audra and *especially* Rosalie asking him the most ridiculous questions. But he handled them all good-naturedly.

And when she'd walked him out to his car that night, he'd kissed her. *Really* kissed her and told her that he was sorry for everything that had happened to her, but he was damn glad she was back in Bent County.

On Valentine's Day, he'd had to work, but he'd sent her flowers and Magnolia a teddy bear. The next day, he took her out to a fancy restaurant in Fairmont.

When she'd let him sweet-talk her into going back to his house for a while, she wondered if maybe fate just got lost sometimes. Or to balance some karmic table, you had to go through the unthinkable to get…this.

But every time she saw his badge, or his gun, or someone called him detective, she got that cold feeling of dread and told herself she was going to break it off.

She didn't. Weeks went by and she didn't. She told herself there'd be a sign, that was when she'd know it was time to go.

But he never bad-talked Rosalie or Audra or Franny,

never resented the time she spent with them or Magnolia. He wasn't perfect. He was terrible with time management, almost always late to pick her up on their dates. Sometimes if work called during a date, he got distracted. Or if a case was particularly frustrating, she might not hear from him except for very rote texts for a day or two.

But the thing was, he was never mean. Never cruel. Not to her or anyone around them.

Because while Eric had kept a lot of his horrible traits under wraps until they were married, there had been signs she hadn't recognized when they'd been dating. Separating her from her family, making it clear he didn't like them. Making sure his criticisms were carefully wrapped up in pretending to care about her. Pulling the silent treatment, then love-bombing her into oblivion.

He hadn't physically hurt her until after the *I dos* had been said, when she'd felt trapped into trying to make it work for far too long.

So Vi kept vigilant. She waited. For the commentary or criticism to start. For it to feel familiar. For her apprehensions about what being a cop did to a guy to be true in Thomas.

They weren't.

She didn't know what to do with falling in love with him all over again, with watching him be amazing with Magnolia. And every time she told herself to stop this ridiculousness, she wondered why.

Why shouldn't she have a great boyfriend who was so good with her daughter? Why shouldn't Magnolia have that kind of positive male influence in her life? Magnolia deserved the *world*, and Vi had already made so many mistakes that might negatively impact her, how could she not want everything for her baby?

Besides, if it didn't work out, if the cop thing became a problem, Magnolia wouldn't even remember.

Vi convinced herself of that.

And still, months went by. Thomas never showed any "true colors," and Vi fell more and more in love with him by the day. He became part of her life again, and part of Magnolia's, and the one thing she kept waiting for—him to push her to talk about her marriage—didn't come.

One night, curled up together on the porch swing after a family dinner and putting Magnolia down together, she wasn't that shocked to hear him say the words, *I love you, Vi.*

For a second, it felt like they could erase fifteen years.

But they couldn't.

"You've held off saying that because you want to know about my marriage."

There was a pause. "Ouch," he said, with a self-deprecating laugh. "Didn't know I was that transparent."

He wasn't. Not really. But she *knew* him.

"You don't have to tell me," he said.

She knew he meant it. He wanted to know, but he wasn't going to manipulate it out of her. It just wasn't *him*, and as much as she still doubted herself sometimes, she could never find the well of distrust within her to not trust Thomas.

So she took a deep breath, and did the unthinkable. She went back to where it all began.

"He never hit me before we got married."

Thomas was very still. He didn't say anything. Just watched her with those patient eyes. Kind eyes.

Because didn't it mean Eric won *again* if she didn't believe any man could be kind, just because she'd had rotten taste in the man she'd agreed to marry?

"I always feel like I have to start with that."

"You don't have to defend yourself to me, Vi. I've seen…

plenty," he said after considering that last word. "I know it's not simple."

She nodded a little, grateful for that. An open-mindedness, even if it reminded her that not everyone who responded to domestic calls had that kind of empathy or ability to see a gray area.

"And he was good at…charming *some* people. My mom loved him. My dad didn't, but you know my dad."

"He's not going to like anyone who touches you."

She snorted a laugh. There was this strange, stabilizing comfort in the fact that he'd known her *before*. That maybe, just maybe, he saw her as the Vi she'd been back then. And she wasn't that girl anymore, but she liked to think she was getting back some of that old confidence and strength.

"Yeah. In fairness, my stepmom didn't like him either. But my friends were split. And it's not like he's the reason I dropped out of premed. I couldn't pass those stupid chemistry classes. Sometimes I think, that's really where it started. I'd felt smart and successful and important my whole life, and I couldn't make it through my freshman year requirements and keep my scholarship."

It still burned. Even after all these years. What a failure she'd made of her chance at something…great.

"I dropped out of Clemson. We couldn't afford it without the scholarship. My dad and stepmom wanted me to get into a nursing program, so I did. But I felt…like a failure. And that made it more of a struggle than it needed to be. Especially when it came to taking the licensing tests. I just…" It still hurt. The way one failure had started a domino effect of self-doubt and no self-esteem. "I was too scared to take them."

"You'd make a great nurse, Vi."

He said that like she still had some kind of chance at

something like that. And the craziest part was believing him. Maybe...maybe she could go back to school. Maybe she *could* be a nurse. Wouldn't that be a great thing for Mags to grow up and see?

"Maybe," she said, because she didn't want to get excited about it until she figured out the logistics. She wasn't *young* anymore. She was a mother. And she still had to tell this awful story.

"I coasted for a long while. Waitressing and just, honestly? Getting more and more depressed. I isolated myself from my friends, from my family, because I felt like such a failure. And then I met Eric. He seemed like a great guy. Funny and fun. And really into me. I felt like I needed that. Someone who didn't look at me and seem disappointed."

He didn't have to say anything to know he wouldn't have been disappointed in her. Then or now. But he hadn't been there, and she'd felt surrounded by people who thought she'd failed.

"He really pursued me, and it made me feel...special. Which I hadn't felt in years. I look back and I think...he knew just who to target. Someone who needed an ego boost. Someone who'd be grateful for any positives."

"That is generally how it goes," Thomas said quietly. Not passing judgment. Just agreeing with her. And still, with her curled up against him, his arm tight around her, like none of this changed anything.

God, she hoped it wouldn't.

"He was like this up-and-coming SWAT team guy, and he didn't need a successful girlfriend. He needed a wife who would support him. So, when he asked me to marry him, I figured I'd throw myself into that. His schedule was crazy. His work demanding and stressful. He used that excuse a lot. Once we were married. Once he started hitting me. I knew it was wrong, but I felt like if I gave up, it was another failure."

Thomas's palm rubbed up and down her arm, and for the first time while going over this she didn't feel shoved back into that place. Of helplessness. Of failure. She could actually look back on it as a past version of herself. A victim, yes.

But now she was a survivor.

"So what changed?" he asked gently.

"Magnolia. The day I found out I was pregnant, I had a black eye and a bruised rib. Eric didn't want kids, but I didn't know what I was more scared of. His reaction if I told him, or his reaction if I decided what to do about it on my own."

She could still feel echoes of that old fear. That complete powerlessness. Knowing she wanted her child and knowing she didn't have any real say. It had been a breaking point.

"Even if he'd let me keep a baby, I just... I remembered how awful it was to be a kid whose parents screamed at each other. I couldn't imagine how much worse it would have been if my dad had ever physically hurt my mom. I didn't want that for any child of mine, and I wanted her. So badly I wanted...to be a mother. To love someone."

He held her tighter against him. "You said, back when Rosalie first had me come out, you said he tried to have you committed."

"I called in a report that day. At first, the officers who responded took me very seriously. But as the days went on, I heard more about how I'd waited. How the prosecutor wouldn't take on a case like mine. I knew Eric was making sure everyone thought I was lying."

Thomas's expression was mostly blank, but she saw in the way he held his jaw, tight and hard, he wasn't just *ab-*

sorbing this information. It bothered him. She supposed she couldn't be hurt by that.

"The next time he hit me, I called the police right away. He didn't even stop me. I thought... I don't know, I really thought that would be it. But he just laughed and told me he'd always win. I didn't know how at the time, but then the cops showed up. They knew him, of course. And when he said I'd hurt myself, that I was a danger to him and myself, that I should be involuntarily committed and he'd be *sure* I got the help I needed, I realized there was no real end. He had all the power."

"He doesn't," Thomas said firmly. Then he relaxed a little, as if he was trying to make himself. "But you figured that out. You left."

"It was my word against theirs, and there was no proof, so they couldn't involuntarily commit me. But I knew if he got another chance, he'd make it happen. They made us separate for the night. And I just took that as my opportunity to run. I went to my dad. I was afraid... Well, I thought maybe he wouldn't help, but it was my only chance."

"I know your dad wasn't perfect, but he did love you."

Vi nodded, trying to blink back tears. "Yeah. Him and Suze saved me. They got me a divorce lawyer. At first, I thought it would be enough." She shook her head, swallowing at the lump in her throat. "Stuff started happening at Dad's house. Tires slashed. Mailboxes knocked over. Little petty things, and no way of proving it was Eric."

"But of course it was Eric."

"Yeah. Luckily, they served him the divorce papers at work. Apparently it was embarrassing enough for him that he got his own lawyer. They somehow made it look like he'd wanted the divorce first. Tried to make it out like I was unstable and a danger to *him*. I didn't even care at that point. Whatever got me out, especially if he never knew I was pregnant. But it left me flat broke, and too close. I couldn't stand the idea of Dad and Suze getting hurt just for helping me, so I was going to leave."

She inhaled, just as her therapist told her. Breathe in and let it all out. Feel your body. Know you're safe.

"Dad insisted on helping me, and I didn't have a choice. I had no money. No…anything. So first, they got me on a flight to Suze's sister in Chicago. Then my aunt and uncle in Phoenix. My aunt and uncle drove me up to Denver, and Audra and Rosalie picked me up there. We thought he wouldn't find me."

"How long did it take?"

"It was almost six months before he called my new number. Every time I'd change it, he'd find it sooner. But it was just…messages about how I was nothing. How much better his life was without me. How he'd won. It's all kind of a blur. Magnolia was born two months early, and I was more focused on that than what messages he left."

"Has he ever threatened Magnolia?"

"I never told him I was pregnant. I didn't go to the doctor until I got out. He doesn't know she exists."

Thomas was clearly confused by this. "If he's gone through the trouble of phone numbers and email addresses, don't you think he knows you had a kid?"

She hesitated for the first time since she'd started. Because the next bit was…well, illegal. "Let's just say…it wasn't exactly… I didn't perhaps give the hospital the full truth."

He frowned at her. "You can tell me, Vi. I'm not going to arrest you."

He seemed irritated enough by the idea, so she figured he deserved the full truth. "Audra… She had me use all her information. Name. Social. Insurance. If anyone looks at Magnolia's birth certificate, they'd think Audra was her mother."

He inhaled slowly, let it out. She couldn't really decide what he thought about any of that, but she'd told him. It was all out there. Whatever happened from here on out was with the whole true story between them.

If he balked now, that was on *him*. She really tried to convince herself it would be on him.

"And that's the whole story?" he asked.

"Pretty much every terrible detail. He calls and leaves a message from time to time or writes an all-caps email from some fake email address. He's usually drunk when he does it. And maybe they sometimes have gotten a little threatening, but he's never left Richmond. Never come looking for me. It's just…him convincing himself he can still mess up my life. He can't."

"No, he can't." Thomas reached out, tucked a strand of hair behind her ear. "I need you to tell me when it happens. Even if it's not a threat. Even if we then pretend it never happened. I need to know."

She didn't like that but was trying to let this relationship be the real deal. Which meant listening to her therapist, not *reacting*, but dealing. Not retreating but putting herself in another person's shoes.

And Thomas dealt with this kind of thing. The crushing regularity of a man who terrorized his significant other. So how could she keep something like that from him?

As much as she wanted to. "If it makes you feel any better, I promised Rosalie and Audra too. Back on that night you came over. I know it's hard to believe, but I… As much shame as I'm still working through, I *am* working through it. I know it's not my fault, what happened to me is not my own failure to hide. Or I'm working on knowing it."

"Vi. That's a lot of important words, but none of them are *I promise*."

She studied his face. The faint hint of whiskers from a long day. The lines around his mouth and eyes now. But those eyes were exactly the same. Blue and earnest and in love with *her*.

She cupped his face with her hands, pressed her mouth to his. "I promise," she managed to say, through a too tight throat.

"I love you, Vi. Call it old, call it new. I don't really care. It's all there."

She hadn't expected *that*, but maybe she should have. "I'm not sure I'm ever going to be okay with you being a cop."

He sucked in a breath, pained. Like she'd stabbed him clean through. Still, he didn't yell. He didn't withdraw or get cold. He just nodded.

Because he *wasn't* Eric. No matter how she kept waiting for her judgment to be wrong, but this wasn't just any guy.

It was Thomas Hart. The first boy she'd loved, and she still recognized that boy, but he was settled in a strong, mature man who'd seen his fair share of bad.

"But I do love you, Thomas."

He studied her face a long time. "I just want you to be happy, Vi."

She thought about her life. Living out here on the ranch and taking care of the ranch. Watching Magnolia grow. Falling in love with her sweet high school boyfriend who maybe had a job that terrified her but was still the same good person she'd loved as a boy.

Two years ago, she'd had no hope she'd ever experience happiness again, and these days she felt it more than all the other things.

"I am happy, Thomas. Very happy."

Chapter Five

He was late, and Thomas *hated* running late for work. Or he had, before Vi. Spending the night out on the Young Ranch tended to override that worry over it. Still, this morning he rushed into the station, offered half-hearted greetings before making it to his office.

God, he needed some coffee. Maybe five minutes to get his thoughts in order. Did he have strained carrots on his pants from feeding Mags this morning?

Laurel was sitting at the desk they had to share. She had been back from maternity leave for a while now, and as Thomas had predicted, the sheriff had expanded the detective department rather than send Copeland back to the road. They had the caseload for it these days.

Laurel looked up at him, then the clock on the wall. "I want to meet her."

She'd hinted, suggested, tried to trick him, but he still hadn't introduced her to Vi. Laurel was five years older than them, so while Vi might have known *of* Laurel Delaney since the Delaneys were a big deal in Bent, Laurel didn't remember Vi.

"Hell no."

"Why not?"

Thomas grinned at her, hanging his bag up on the hook

behind the door. "Because it's driving you crazy." And because he tried to keep all the *cop* parts of his life away from Vi. Even if it was hard. Even if it hurt.

But love was a hell of a thing. He'd keep a million things out of her way if it meant waking up with her every morning. Putting Mags to bed at night together. He'd sacrifice a million things for those quiet, perfect moments.

"I've never seen you this happy," Laurel said, a bit like an accusation.

Thomas didn't know what to say to that, since it was true. So he just grunted.

When Copeland walked into the detective office, blissfully later than Thomas himself, Laurel jabbed a finger at him. "Has *he* met her?"

"No."

"Well, that's something." Laurel and Copeland had learned how to deal with each other, but Thomas wouldn't call it an *easy* relationship. Neither one of them quite trusted the other yet, but Thomas figured it would come with time. They were both too good professionally to let oil and water personalities get in the way for long.

"Look, she's a homebody and she's got a one-year-old." Thomas shrugged. "We just don't get out much."

Laurel pointed a finger at him. "Play date."

"No."

"My kids are desperate to meet new kids."

"Your kids have three million cousins their age to play with. Besides, Mags is just starting to walk. She doesn't need your brood running her over."

"Mags?"

"It's short for Magnolia," he muttered. "Now can I have my desk? I've got that report to finalize."

"*Our* desk, buddy." But she got up.

It was indeed *their* desk, because littered across it were pictures of the Delaney-Carsons. For a moment, Thomas was distracted not by the old, vague sense of envy, but a new one of how that *could* be his future.

Future being the operative word. Because it had only been a few months. Even if fifteen years before, it had been four years. But they'd been different then. Everything had been different.

When he caught Laurel staring at him, probably because he'd been staring at her pictures, he ignored it and got to work.

Later when they ate their lunches in the office, discussing Copeland's current robbery case, Vicky stuck her head in the door.

"This was delivered to the front desk for you, Hart," Vicky said. She tossed a slim envelope onto his desk.

He set his sub sandwich aside and lifted the envelope. The return address was a police department in Texas. "We had any dealing with someone in Plano?" he asked offhandedly, breaking the seal.

"Not that I recall," Laurel replied.

Inside the envelope was a stack of pictures. He frowned at the first one. It was kind of grainy, the lighting not very good, but he recognized that wavy red hair.

Everything inside him went utterly still at the trickle of blood running down her nose.

With a slight tremor in his hands, he flipped to the next picture. A close-up this time, still grainy. A black eye, dark and big.

Every single one featured Vi. With a bruise or injury somewhere on her body. And with each picture, his blood ran more and more cold. He reached the end of the stack, expecting some kind of note, some kind of *something*.

But there was nothing but the pictures. Thomas was on his feet, the chair clattering behind him, without a thought to Copeland or Laurel asking him what was wrong. Nothing mattered but getting to Vi.

But there she was. In the doorway. No bruises. No visible injuries. But she was pale.

And clutching an envelope to her chest that looked just like the one on his desk.

THREE SETS OF eyes were on her, but Vi only noticed Thomas's. Worry and anger. She saw the envelope on his desk that looked just like the one that had been in the mail this afternoon.

Eric had sent Thomas pictures too.

Oh, *God*. For a second, she thought her knees might buckle. She shouldn't have come to his work. She shouldn't have come. She shouldn't have.

He skirted the desk so quickly, she didn't even have time to flinch when he grabbed her. But it wasn't a *grab*, or at least not the kind her body was preparing for. He hugged her. Tight and close.

She felt her knees sag. Fear had propelled her from the ranch all the way to the Bent County Police Station, but Thomas's strong arms around her was like a wake-up call.

"Thomas, I have to..." Run. Just *run*.

"Let me see the envelope," he said, carefully loosening his grip but only just, so enough space remained between them to take it out of her hands. When he held it out, the woman who'd been in the office with him—no doubt Laurel the detective he occasionally talked about—had a bag open and he dropped the envelope in.

"Copeland?" he said.

The man was another detective Vi knew just from putting little clues together, because Thomas didn't talk about his job much. Purposefully. He had taken her *I'm not sure I'm ever going to be okay with you being a cop* to heart and did everything he could to keep that life separate from theirs.

For a moment, that felt like another pain, just to go along with all the others. Another failure in the never-ending cascade of them.

She closed her eyes, took a deep breath. Those knee-jerk meltdowns would probably never go away, but she wouldn't let them sabotage the life she was building.

Copeland took the bag with her envelope in it, while holding another bag with an identical envelope in it.

"I'll get them processed and printed." He nodded at her, intense and direct. The female detective—short, blond, pretty, no doubt Laurel—was watching Thomas.

Thomas kept his arm around Vi, but moved so they were more hip to hip. "Copeland will see if we can get a print, more information on where they came from," he said. He pointed to the woman. "This is my other partner, Laurel Delaney-Carson."

Vi nodded, beyond uncomfortable his coworkers were witnessing this…awful, awful thing. She didn't want them seeing the pictures. She didn't want Laurel, this person she *knew* Thomas looked up to, seeing…all her failures.

Not failures, Vi. Don't let him win this.

"I'll give you two some privacy," Laurel said with a kind smile. "You let me know if I can be of any help." Then she left.

Thomas rubbed his hand up and down her arm. "Did you drive out here? Where's Mags?"

"Franny's got her. I didn't want to… I was going to call you, but I didn't want you coming to the ranch, bringing all

this ugliness out there more than it already is. I couldn't..."
She wouldn't cry. She just wouldn't allow herself to do that
here. Maybe once she was back in her car alone. Definitely
tonight in bed. Alone.

Because how could she keep doing this thing with Thomas
with this hanging over her head?

Eric had sent him those pictures too. A new bolt of fear
struck her at her core. Eric had never involved anyone else
once she'd left her father's house. All his threats were to
her and her alone.

But if he knew she was dating Thomas... If he was threatening *him* by sending these pictures...

She turned to face Thomas again, grabbed on to him.
He was real, he was strong. But... "If he sent them to you,
this is more. It's... He can't come here. He can't know about
Magnolia. He can't—"

Thomas took her hands in his. Squeezed. "So he won't."

His gaze was so direct. So sure.

She wished she could believe his certainty. But she'd
once been certain. She'd once believed all it would take
was going to the police to save her from Eric.

She'd been so wrong. "Thomas. I have to leave. I have
to run. If he comes here..."

"You will be protected."

"I don't think you understand," she said, trying to maintain her calm, her composure. She had to be composed or
he'd look at her and see everything those other cops had seen.

Hysteria. Overreaction.

"It's not like I just ran. That was a last resort. I tried to
tell people. I tried to get help. But his entire precinct believed him, supported him. He was *this* close to having me
involuntarily committed. If I hadn't run away, he would
have made it happen."

Or maybe he would have killed me. She knew how possible it was. How likely he would have been to get away with it.

"This is Bent County. He doesn't control us."

"But you could control them if you wanted to." She hated the words the *second* they were out her mouth. She squeezed her eyes shut. "I'm sorry. I know you don't deserve that."

"No, I suppose I don't." Then his arms were around her, pulling her close. Gently this time. "But you didn't deserve what happened to you. Life isn't fair. We know that."

Chapter Six

Thomas had been shot. He'd been injured a number of times in the line of duty. Hell, he'd lived through Vi breaking his heart once before. It wasn't like he couldn't live through her saying stuff like that.

He knew it wasn't about *him*. It was about the hell she'd lived through. Survived. Escaped. But it was never going to be past tense as long as her ex-husband had the means to reach her like this.

He pulled her back by the shoulders, ignored the hurt on his heart, and looked her dead in the eye. "You were right to run the first time, because he'd isolated you and you didn't have a choice. But you ran to your dad because you knew he would help. Now you ran to me, because you know I'll help. Who else is there to run to, Vi? Who else has a better chance of keeping you safe?"

He could see the push and pull in her expression. She wanted him to protect her. But she couldn't quite let herself believe he would, or could.

But this was not about their relationship, his ego, or anything about them on a personal level. It was about a threat.

"Thomas, I don't want you stepping in the middle and getting hurt."

"Why the hell not?" he demanded, with enough heat that she winced and he hated himself.

He took a deep breath, gentled his tone. "Vi, I took an oath when I put on that badge. And it involves laying my life down for the law, for the citizens of this county. If I'd do that for a stranger, I'm sure as hell going to do it for the people I love."

She was shaking her head, but the hell with that.

"It doesn't matter whether I love you or not, Vi. That's how I'd feel. You could be a stranger bringing me a case, and I'd damn well be getting to the bottom of it, regardless of the danger. That's my job. That's an oath I took. That's who I am."

And that was hard to say. Not because it wasn't true, but because if she couldn't accept that, he didn't know how to move forward. He could overlook a lot, compartmentalize almost everything. But not this.

"So there's no point in arguing this," he said, trying not to sound as destroyed as he felt. He dropped her shoulders, settled a hip back on his desk. "Walk me through getting that envelope. Start at the beginning."

She looked at him, too many heartbreaks to name in those dark blue eyes. But he couldn't let that sway him. If he was going to promise her he'd do this for anyone, then he had to do this like he'd do it for anyone.

She was quiet for so long, he thought she might not say anything. He thought...maybe, this was a wall he couldn't get through. And then what? How did he proceed knowing she was in danger? Knowing she didn't want his help?

"Audra came in for lunch and brought the mail like she always does," she finally said, her voice rough.

A weaker man might have collapsed to the floor at the

sheer weight lifted from his entire being, but Thomas held himself firm.

"That envelope was in with the other mail. She asked me if I knew anyone in Texas. I don't. So we opened it together. I made it through…two or three pictures before I stopped looking. I don't know how many Audra looked at."

"Then what?"

"I knew I had to bring them to you. I didn't want you coming out to the ranch. Maybe I should have. Maybe they're in danger. Maybe…"

He reached out and took her hand, couldn't stop himself from offering some physical comfort. "Let's not deal in maybes, sweetheart. Let's focus on what you did. You had Franny watch Mags and you got in your car and drove straight out here?"

She nodded.

"No stops? Just right here?"

She nodded again. He supposed it soothed something inside of him that her first instinct, even if she'd since questioned it, was to come to him.

"Before this, how long has it been since you'd heard from him? Phone. Email. Whatever. I know there was the phone call a few months back when Rosalie first told me about all this. Anything between then and now?"

She blinked, got a slightly confused expression on her face. "No, of course not. I would have told you."

Relief was wrong to feel right now, with so many unknowns around them, but it *was* a relief. If she could trust him enough to tell him, to be confused he might even think she wouldn't, they could get through this. He was sure of it.

He was going to be sure of it.

"I want to listen to those voicemails. Read those emails. From the beginning."

"I deleted them," she said, with a bit of a wince again. Like she expected him to explode. "I think Rosalie made copies, though."

"I'm going to drive you back to the ranch. We're going to tell everyone there what happened. I'm going to take a statement from Audra. I'm going to see what Rosalie has on the past threats—no doubt her own case file."

"But..." She looked around his office. "You're working."

"Yes, I am working. This is my case now."

"Thomas, you can't—"

"I can. I'm going to." On that, he wouldn't take no for an answer. "I'm going to need to bring in Laurel or Copeland. Do you have a preference? Some women prefer to work with Laurel."

"Can't it just be you? I..." She looked at the door that Laurel had closed behind her when she left. "I don't know these people. I can't..."

"For a lot of reasons, I need more hands and eyes than mine." He stood behind her, wrapped his arms around her and held on. Because he needed to, and when she leaned into him, relaxed her shoulders a bit, he knew she needed it too. "But the main reason is I want someone else's opinion. I want to make sure I'm not missing anything."

"I guess, whichever one you trust the most then."

"I trust them both, Vi. I need you to know that. I won't put your case in anyone's hands I don't trust with my own life."

She'd stiffened a little but didn't pull away. She just nodded. He gave her one last squeeze, released her. "Give me a few minutes, then we'll head back to the ranch."

"Okay."

He left her in his office, but he closed the door so she could feel like she had some privacy. He found Laurel alone in an interrogation room, going over some paperwork. She looked up when he came in, and he saw sympathy in her gaze.

"You looked at the pictures."

"Yeah. I assume she knows the asshole who did that to her?"

"Ex-husband. Some SWAT guy in Virginia who basically had his whole precinct eating out of his hand and not believing her. I have a bad feeling we're not going to be able to find proof he sent those pictures, but it's a starting point to end this for her. I'm going to the Young Ranch to get official statements from Audra Young. I'm also going to talk to all the other residents. I want your help on this, but more on the periphery. She doesn't trust cops, and who could blame her?"

Laurel nodded. "Okay, I'll let you know when we get the results on the envelope and pictures. Any other cases you want to hand off to me or Copeland, just say the word. Focus on this one for right now."

There'd been no doubt Laurel would understand, that she'd have his back and give him what he needed. And still, he was just...relieved. At anything that went right, he was going to be grateful.

"Keep me updated, and let us know if you need anything else," she said.

"Yeah. Thanks."

"We'll get to the bottom of it," Laurel said, reassuringly. "We've always got your back, Hart."

He knew they did, particularly Laurel who'd been his first training officer. She was the one who'd recommended him to take over as detective when she'd been on her first maternity leave. She'd been a mentor from day one, and she'd become as close as a sister to him.

But with Vi and Magnolia's safety on the line, her words didn't reassure.

No one's could.

THOMAS DROVE VI back to the ranch in her car. When she asked how he'd get back to Bent, he told her he'd handle it.

She believed he would and could, even with fear and nerves and embarrassment and a hundred other terrible feelings battling it out inside of her. She knew that Thomas was more than capable of handling all this.

It was strange. So strange it almost felt *wrong*. Because she'd spent her whole life being the one who figured out how to handle it. While her parents had been acting like spoiled children when she was a kid—using her like some kind of bargaining chip in a failing marriage. When she'd gone off to Clemson thinking she knew how the world worked and how her future would pan out. Even when she'd been married to Eric, who'd been controlling in a way that at first had almost made her feel safe and protected and not the one who had to *do* everything, eventually she'd started to feel like the only one who could hold it all together. Like the fate of her life rested on every single minute decision she made.

Her cousins, Franny, they had all been amazing since she'd made it out here. They'd helped so much, especially when Mags had been in the NICU, but even then, Vi had insisted on handling as much as she could on her own. Only in the past few months had she really started to relent. To Audra and Rosalie, to Franny, to Thomas.

Her therapist said it was healthy, but now it seemed dangerous. Like every step forward was drawing more people into the hell she'd escaped. If this was just about her, she probably would have bolted. Even now, she considered it.

Audra had every legal right to raise Magnolia. If Vi just disappeared...

"I need you to promise me one thing in all of this, Vi."

Vi blinked out of her whirling thoughts, looked at Thomas. His expression was grim as he drove. "What's that?"

"You'll be honest with me, no matter what. With anything that happens, with what you're feeling. Any contact that feels off. If you're considering running. Just tell me."

Could he read her mind? Was she that transparent? Or did he just understand, because he dealt with *victims* like her, all the time? And there was something about that awful thought—that she was just like the people he helped—that had her saying the truth.

"I'll probably consider running every day."

He glanced at her once, oh-so-serious. "It would break my heart if you did."

A quick, painful stab went right in her own heart. "That's not fair."

His mouth quirked up on the side as he looked back at the road. "I know. That's why I said it. I'm not above being unfair to keep you safe."

"I just don't want anyone else paying for a mistake I made."

"So, let me handle this for you, Vi. And there won't be mistakes."

She wondered if the confidence was natural, something born from all the work he'd done, or something he was putting on to settle her, but it worked.

When they got to the ranch and went inside, Thomas talked to everyone and Vi got Magnolia down for her nap. She knew she should go see what Thomas was saying to everyone, but instead she just watched her daughter sleep.

For over a year, she'd been running. Hiding. For over a

year, she'd spent time healing herself, but there'd always been this little part of her—the *victimized* part, she could accept now—that was waiting.

Waiting to be hurt again.

Waiting to run.

She'd known this moment was coming.

Thomas slid into the room. He came to stand next to her, wrapped his arm around her. He looked down at Mags, fast asleep in her crib. And Vi saw one of the things she'd first allowed herself to recognize about Thomas.

He loved her daughter.

"I want you to come stay in town with me for a little bit," he whispered, tearing his gaze from Mags to her. "The ranch is too big. My house is small. I've got great neighbors who know who should be coming and going and are just busybodies enough to let me know. I've got some security, and a friend who can bulk it up."

"What about Audra, Rosalie and Franny?"

"I talked to them. Audra said she's going to talk to the neighbors, ask that anyone who sees something off to let them know. Rosalie's going to put up some cameras she uses for work. She also informed me they are 'armed to the teeth,' which I can't say made me feel great. I'll have whatever manpower I can manage check in throughout the day, drive by at night."

Vi tried not to feel like she'd ruined everyone's life. Made everything ten times more difficult on the people who'd helped her through the worst.

"Everyone is happy to rally around you, Vi. You and Mags. Because they—because *we* want what you want. This life you've built. For you. For Magnolia. We want you to have it, and we want to be a part of your life."

Vi looked down at her sleeping daughter, felt the easy

strength of Thomas next to her. Thought about this life—and he was right, she'd *built* it. Out of the wreckage of her old one, with the help of her loved ones, *for* her daughter.

Her daughter, who called Thomas *Tata*. Magnolia loved him. And her honorary aunts. Audra was Aw. Rosalie, Ee. Franny, for some inexplicable reason, was Geen. She'd taken her first steps in this ranch house and was thriving. After all the NICU business, she was *thriving*.

So Vi met Thomas's gaze and nodded. Yes, this was the life she wanted for her daughter.

"So, we'll fight for it. Together."

For the first time since she'd gotten those pictures, Vi thought...maybe they could.

Chapter Seven

After Mags woke up from her nap, they packed up a few things and Thomas drove Vi and Magnolia back to his house.

Zach's truck was still out front when they got there. "Do you mind meeting some friends of mine?"

Vi grimaced, but she nodded. "Oh. Well. Okay."

They got out of the car, just as Zach was coming out of the front door. He was grappling with his very energetic three-year-old, Cooper.

"Hart. Ma'am."

"Zach, this is Vi Reynolds. Vi, this is Zach Simmons. A friend of mine, and he has a security business with Cam Delaney, Laurel's brother."

"Hi," Vi offered.

"Nice to meet you, Vi. I'd shake your hand, but if I let him go, he's going to bolt."

"I'm a dinosaur!" Cooper shouted. Then gave an impressive roar. Magnolia stared down at him dubiously and clutched onto Vi tighter.

"I checked out the security system," Zach said, while Cooper grumbled and tried to escape the hold Zach had on him. "Should be able to get everything upgraded by tomorrow. Mostly done through my computer, but Cam or I might need to stop by tomorrow to do some on-site stuff."

"Thanks, man."

"Any time." He wrangled his wriggly toddler. "Lucy's inside. She wanted to make everything look nice." Zach rolled his eyes. But as if on cue, Lucy came out the front door and walked up to them.

Vi's eyes got real wide. It was kind of funny, Lucy had been a fixture around Bent for enough years now that Thomas forgot to a lot of people, she was someone else. Before anyone could make introductions, Vi spoke.

"You're...Daisy Delaney," Vi said, clear awe in her tone.

Lucy clearly wasn't surprised by it. She no doubt got that just about everywhere she went outside of Bent. "I just go by Lucy around here."

"You... I listen to your...music. All the time."

"Good to hear," Lucy said. She stood next to Zach, gave the wriggling toddler one quelling look and Cooper stopped trying to escape his dad's hold. "And who's this?" she asked, reaching out and giving Magnolia's hand a little shake.

Vi looked down at the daughter on her hip. "Magnolia. I... I named her after your song."

Lucy's smile widened. "Isn't that something?" She studied Magnolia in Vi's arms. "I miss this age. If you can't tell, our three-year-old is like a human wrecking ball."

"And just moved to a toddler bed. So they're letting us borrow some things while you're staying here," Thomas said. "Crib. High chair. We should be all set."

"Oh, well, thank you. I... That's so nice."

"No worries." Lucy patted her tiny baby bump. "We'll need them back in a few months, but for now, they're all yours. We've had them in storage anyway while we're redoing our house."

"We'll leave you to it, but if you need anything else, let

us know," Zach said. He started moving for his truck, but Lucy didn't. She pointed at Thomas.

"You're coming to Cam and Hilly's baby shower, right?"

Thomas tried not to sigh. "Yeah, if I can swing it."

"Bring the whole gang," she said, smiling at Vi and Mags. "The more the merrier. Hope to see you there, Vi." She had to speak louder with every sentence over Cooper's roaring.

Magnolia reached out for Thomas, so he took her. She snuggled in. "Not sure Mags was a fan of Cooper," he said, holding her close. "Come on, sweets," he walked up to his front door, ushered Vi in.

"I don't need to go," Vi said. "To the baby shower," she added, when it was clear he'd lost the thread.

"Oh, if I'm going, you're going," Thomas said. He'd forgotten about the co-ed baby shower. His least favorite kind of forced party. Weddings and adult bridal showers at least usually had some alcoholic social lubricant, and kids' birthday parties were easy to hide in, what with all the screeching and sugar.

"But I don't even know these people," Vi continued.

"Good. Then you won't leave my side and I can have an excuse not to play one of those horrible baby shower games."

"Thomas."

He didn't quite know why she'd not want to come, except maybe she thought it was a cop thing. "Cam and Hilly aren't cops. Zach was FBI, but he just does security now. Laurel will be there, but I think that's about it on the cop front. Cam's her brother, so she'll be too sappy to bring up any shop talk."

"That's not what I'm worried about."

He studied her then. The frustrated look on her face, which poked at his temper when it shouldn't.

It *shouldn't*.

"Then what is?"

She looked up at him, but she didn't answer his question. "I just don't think I should go."

He supposed the fact she wouldn't give him a real answer made him say what he shouldn't. "They're my friends, Vi. And you're my...for lack of a more adult word, girlfriend. I love you. Why wouldn't you want to be part of my life?" And he should not be laying that at her feet after the day she'd had. Before she could say anything, he kept right on, hoping to dig himself out of the hole.

"Look, today's been a lot. It's not the day to have this conversation. Let's have some dinner." He tried to shake his frustration, and holding on to Magnolia helped. "I don't have much. Soup?"

Vi was still standing by the door when he looked back at her, but she'd closed it. She didn't say anything for the longest time. When she finally did, it wasn't at all what he expected.

"You know Daisy Delaney."

"Yeah." She was letting it go. So he smiled at her. "Did I not mention it?"

She scowled at him. "No, you did not."

"I've got all sorts of surprises up my sleeve, Vi."

She grunted, then came over to him. "I'll handle dinner since you've handled just about everything else."

He would have argued, but it seemed like she needed it. And he understood. The desire to *do* something when feeling helpless. He entertained Mags while Vi made them dinner. Then they sat down and ate together.

Which wasn't the first time. They'd been doing this a lot. But out at the ranch. Out in *her* space, with *her* family. This was *his* home and it made it feel like...

They were a family. Which was too soon, he knew. Vi had a lot to work through, and he could be patient.

But it still wound through him like pain, how much he wanted this to be his life. They bathed Mags, put her to bed. Since Magnolia's crib was set up in his bedroom, they made out on the couch in the living room watching a movie like they were teenagers again. There was something kind of fun about that. About forgetting the ugliness she'd been through and just being their old selves for a tiny sliver of time.

When they went to bed, Vi snuggled in next to him like she belonged there. In this life he'd built for himself over the past fifteen years. He wanted that to be the only thing he thought about.

He watched her sleep for a while, trying to see this—the beautiful woman she was, who loved him enough and trusted him enough to let him protect her.

But instead, all he dreamed about were those pictures.

Vi woke up in a foreign bed, late morning sunlight streaming through the curtains. She sat bolt upright in bed, *Thomas's* bed. The crib in the corner was empty, and she looked at the clock.

"Ten?" she screeched. She practically raced out of the bedroom, then skidded to a halt at the sight that greeted her.

Thomas was in the kitchen. He had his work khakis on, but no shirt. One of his county polos was draped over the back of a chair.

He had Magnolia on his hip, bouncing her while she smiled and babbled. The highchair was a mess, so Mags had clearly eaten.

"I did not learn my lesson," he offered to her over his shoulder. "My shirt got peach smushed. Coffee's up."

It was like…all those things she'd imagined married life would be. It was all those things she'd wanted, so much so she'd ignored her intuition over and over again when it came to Eric.

And here it was, in her high school boyfriend. In all the simple things she probably would have scoffed at fifteen years ago. Letting her sleep in. Coffee made. Baby taken care of.

And she wasn't eighteen, or even twenty-four anymore. She was a mother in her thirties. She'd been through hell. And hell wasn't over yet.

But she had to be the one to end it. Once and for all. So she could enjoy all this glorious simple.

She crossed to him, wrapped her arms around him. Enjoyed the strength she found there—physical and otherwise. "I love you very much."

He wound his arm around her, kissed her head. "Well, I love you too."

"And if there's anything I need to do. Answer questions. Get those police reports from Richmond." She swallowed hard at the way her throat closed up at the next suggestion. "Go through each and every one of those pictures with you. Whatever I can do to end this, I will do it. I'm ready to do it."

He studied her a long time, then ran his free hand over her hair. "I'm glad to hear it. Right now, you're just going to sit tight and let me do my job. Okay?"

She nodded, leaned into him. "Okay."

"I'm going to go into the precinct, check up on those prints. The return address. A few other things. Franny is already on her way to hang with you today. I want you to stay close, but don't feel like a prisoner. I'll show you both how to work the security system before I leave. And I'm only a phone call away."

He handed Magnolia off, who wasn't happy with the transfer at all. "Tata!"

"Gotta clean up the mess you made out of me, sweets." Then he gave her a loud kiss on her cheek and disappeared into his bedroom.

For a moment, Vi let herself believe this could be her life. If she could be strong. If she could keep the promises she was making to Thomas.

This could be everything.

The doorbell rang, and Vi opened it up to Franny. Mags squealed in delight and Franny grabbed her enthusiastically. They babbled nonsense at each other, their favorite greeting, and when Thomas came out of the room, he was dressed for work.

He walked Franny and her through his security system, then gave her and Mags a kiss and was off. Vi stood in the doorway watching him go.

When he was out of earshot, she said what the little voice in her head kept insisting. "Am I stupid for trusting him, Franny?"

"You'd be stupid not to, Vi. He's great. He loves you and Mags. And he's going to do everything to protect you. What more could you ask for?"

"What if it's all too good to be true?"

"Seems like if anyone has earned a little too good to be true, it's you. Besides, your ex-husband is harassing you. That's not good."

"No." She closed the door, turned to the living room, Franny by her side. "I'm sorry you're getting dragged into this. You have work to do, I know."

"Are you kidding?" Franny rubbed her hands together.

"This is great research. I'm going to poke around his house and see how a real detective lives."

"You can't snoop."

"Why not?"

"Because..." Vi was sure there were a lot of good reasons why not, but she couldn't think of a one.

"Like, what does a detective keep in his fridge? Am I going to find a Glock hidden in the freezer?"

"I hope not," Vi muttered, watching as Franny went right over to the fridge and looked through its contents.

Vi got out her phone. Opened a text to Thomas. She didn't want him coming home tonight and angry about someone touching and moving his things.

Franny is snooping around your house for research.

His response was almost immediate. That's okay. Nothing to hide. Except in my underwear drawer.

Something inside of her eased, and she realized she sometimes—without realizing it—still expected him to react like Eric would. Which wasn't fair, and she hated that it still snuck up on her.

She typed her response firmly, wanting to focus on Thomas and Thomas alone. And what's in your underwear drawer?

Guess you'll have to snoop and find out.

She didn't. She wasn't going to. She trailed after Franny while Franny went through his kitchen drawers, bathroom cabinets. While she complained about how *normal* his stuff was.

And then, when Franny had settled herself in Thomas's

office, Vi quietly left the room and went to Thomas's bedroom with Magnolia on her hip.

"He basically told me to," she said to Mags. She carefully opened the top drawer of his dresser. Maybe it was a joke. Maybe…

But there in the far corner was a little prayer book, of all things. When she opened it up, she saw the inscription. *To Thomas, From Grandma.* His Grandma Hart had been very religious. She'd passed away their senior year, and Thomas had been devastated. Vi remembered going to the funeral.

It was one of the few times she'd thought staying in Bent wouldn't be so bad. To be part of a community that rallied around, that grieved together. Then she'd gone home that night to her mom, who was passed out drunk while one of her boyfriends rifled through her purse.

She'd only thought about getting out from there after that.

Magnolia reached out and swatted the book. "Gentle," Vi said quietly.

She didn't think this was what he'd been talking about in his text. Not when she flipped through the pages and a picture fell out.

Their senior prom picture. Her terrible eyeliner, his baby face. But so ridiculously in love. So happy.

"Ma," Magnolia said, bouncing happily.

Tears filled Vi's eyes, but she blinked them back. "Yes, that's Mama. And Tata."

Because Franny was right.

They all deserved a little too good to be true.

Chapter Eight

Maybe Thomas shouldn't have come into the department today. Even after adjusting his hours for the late morning, he wanted to snap just about everyone's head off.

The prints weren't ready. There was no information from the Texas police precinct. No one had any answers, and no one seemed that keen on getting them.

Which he knew was not a fair characterization. Police work was slow, methodical, and rushing things didn't help solve any cases.

But damn, he wanted to rush. He didn't like this hanging over their heads for a lot of reasons, but doing slow, methodical *waiting* while Vi and Magnolia were back at his house, even with Franny, really grated.

Her ex-husband sending those pictures was an escalation. Likely there'd be a few more before he escalated far enough to actually threaten Vi's physical well-being, but there was a lot of psychological well-being to threaten in the meantime.

Rosalie swanned into his office, clearly not having gone through the front desk. He might have scowled at her, but she dropped a folder on his desk in front of him. "All the emails, and a transcription of all the voicemails she gave me access to. I can email you the file too, but I thought this might be…safer."

Thomas nodded and immediately flipped the folder open. While his email was on the county police server, with lots of security, he didn't know about Rosalie's. "Do you think there are ones she didn't show you?"

Rosalie paused. He wasn't sure if she was deciding on her answer, or on whether to *tell* him her answer, but in the end, she shrugged. "I don't know why she'd let me see some, and not others. Maybe if she didn't have Mags I'd think she was hiding the worst of it from me, but she's going to protect Magnolia at all costs."

Luckily, that lined up with what he thought, but he wanted to hear it from someone who'd been around Vi this past year. "Good."

"I'm glad she's staying with you, because the ranch *is* too big to protect. But it's hardly a long-term solution to have her and Mags at your place."

He looked up, into Rosalie's worried blue eyes. "Why not?"

"We don't know how long this is going to take. That ex-husband has been pretty careful, and this still isn't an actual threat. This could be an ongoing issue. She's been here over a year. Who knows how long it continues. Are you just going to have them permanently move in with you?"

He looked at her evenly and tried not to let it show how much he wanted exactly that. Just not with Vi's ex-husband's threats hanging over their head. "Again," he said, very calmly, "why not?"

She grinned at him. "Just testing you, Hart. She's been through hell. She doesn't need some stupid guy with good intentions stomping on her heart because he's careless. I guess you're not."

"I've never been careless, Rosalie."

"Good." She got to her feet. "I'm doing my own investigation, obviously, but keep me in the loop."

"I guess it would be a waste of breath to tell you to leave it to the police department?"

"It would indeed."

He sighed. "All right. I'll keep you in the loop, if you do the same."

She nodded, then exited the way she'd come. Not a few minutes later, Laurel entered the office, a woman behind her. Mid- to late thirties, dressed professionally in a blazer and a skirt and sensible heels. Not a cop. Maybe a lawyer?

Hell, he did not want to deal with any lawyers today.

"Thomas, this is Postal Inspector Dianne Kay."

Thomas stood, held out his hand and shook hers. After he did, she held out a badge. "I'm out of the Fort Worth, Texas, office. I need to ask you a few questions about an envelope you received in the mail yesterday."

Texas. Envelope.

Suddenly, he was a little more interested in dealing with a postal inspector. "Have a seat," he said, taking his behind the desk. Laurel took a chair toward the side. "You work quick to be up here already."

"We try, but we've been following this for a while now. We're investigating a series of fraudulent uses of the mail. All stemming from the police department in Plano, Texas. I was in Denver yesterday when we got word that another set of envelopes had been flagged by postal employees here in Bent County."

"I did receive an envelope yesterday with a return address of the Plano Police Department."

Inspector Kay nodded. "As far as our investigation is

concerned, no one who works at the Plano Police Department is behind these letters. We're trying to find out who is."

"What were in the other letters?"

She smiled at him. "I think you know I can't tell you that."

Irritation simmered, because she *could* tell him that, if she wanted. She didn't have to play things like that *perfectly* by the book. But if he put up a stink about it, he knew what people would say. That he was too close to the case, and he'd start putting himself in danger of getting taken off it.

He trusted Laurel and Copeland, but that didn't mean he'd be able to handle not being involved.

"Did you keep the envelope and its contents?" she asked.

"They were somewhat threatening in nature, so we're doing some analysis. Once I have the answers, you can take a look at whatever you need to."

"I'm sorry. You can finish your tests, I suppose. But it'll be a little bit more than taking a look. Those objects are now evidence in a *federal* investigation. I'll have to take them."

She said it apologetically, and not like some of the federal agents he dealt with—with a kind of smug superiority. Still, it grated. The last thing he wanted to do was hand it over to someone who had to deal with federal red tape.

"It was addressed to me. The return address had no name. No identifying information. Just the return address of the Plano Police Department."

"I'm going to need the envelope." When Thomas opened his mouth to protest, she kept talking. "I don't need to take it just yet, as I'm planning to stay in Bent a few days, but I do need to see the address now so I can verify."

"Will a photograph work?"

She nodded. He motioned her to come around to his

side of the desk, and he brought up the pictures he'd taken of the envelope.

"Cute. Those your kids?" she asked, pointing at all the picture frames on the desk.

"Oh, no. They're Detective Delaney-Carson's," he said, nodding at Laurel. "We share a desk."

He should put a picture of Vi and Magnolia up too. But for now, he focused on the computer screen. "Here's the return address. The address here, with my name as the addressee."

She had a notebook and was taking notes.

"And the contents?" she asked.

"Pictures."

"Of?"

He didn't want to tell her, but that was silly. Maybe their investigations would line up and this could be over all that much sooner. "A friend of mine. We're working under the theory that they came from her ex-husband."

"I'm going to need the names of both," she said. "Spell them out for me. Any other information you have about either one of them. I'd also like you to email me these," she said, pointing at the computer screen.

With a sick, heavy feeling in his gut, Thomas told her Vi's name, and Eric's. When it came to Eric, Thomas gave her the information Vi had given him yesterday. When it came to Vi...

"Can I get an address?"

He couldn't exactly tell this federal agent the person was living *with* him. Was his *girlfriend*. She wouldn't understand. "It's a ranch out by Sunrise. A ways away. I can give you her phone number."

"That'll work."

He rattled off the number.

The woman pulled a card out of her bag, then scribbled something on the back. "You can email me the photos of the envelope at the email on the front. And there's my cell on the back if you need it."

"Sure. Thanks."

"I'll be back probably around midday tomorrow to collect the evidence. Hopefully I'll have a few more questions for you once I've talked to the names you gave me." She stuffed everything back in her bag. "I don't suppose you know a good place to get dinner around here?"

There was something about the way she said it, smiled with her head cocked so that was just enough warning to tread lightly. That and Laurel's eyebrow raise aimed at him.

Lucky for him, Copeland walked by in the nick of time.

"Hey, Copeland. You know any places the postal inspector could get a decent meal in Fairmont?"

Copeland smiled at Dianne. "Sure. I live out that way. I can give you a few suggestions."

"Detective Beckett is part of our department too," Thomas explained. "Inspector Kay here came up from Texas by way of Denver to investigate some mail fraud with that envelope we got yesterday. Copeland used to be a detective in Denver."

Inspector Kay offered Copeland a bland kind of smile. "Not quite a promotion coming out this way, is it?"

Copeland didn't take any offense to that. He grinned. "Well, I'd love to tell you all about it. There's a pretty decent Italian place. If you're looking for some company, I'm about to clock out. Be happy to take you."

"Oh." She looked back at Thomas, then straightened her shoulders. "Well, thanks, but I think I'll just do some takeout. It's been a long day." She turned back to Thomas, aimed that megawatt smile at him. "I'll be back tomorrow, Detective Hart."

"Sure. I'll be here."

Then the inspector left, leaving the three of them in the detective's office.

"Did you just strike out?" Laurel demanded of Copeland, clearly delighted at the prospect.

"I wasn't batting," Copeland grumbled.

"Like hell you weren't," Laurel said with a laugh. "You asked her out. She said no. Then gave Hart some big eyes."

"Yeah, Hart's a real popular guy these days."

"He finally grew into that baby face," Laurel said, pinching his cheek before Thomas could sidestep her. "You know when he started at the county, he only weighed one-fifty."

"It was more than that," Thomas said, glaring at Laurel. "Maybe we could focus on our case instead of everyone's romantic life?"

"What romantic life?" Copeland demanded. "She's saddled with four kids, and you're hog-tied and babysitting."

"Trust me, Beckett. My husband could make a life with *ten* kids romantic. You should be so lucky." She gave him a little nudge so she could move around him. "I'm clocked out. See you tomorrow, boys."

"You clocking out too?" Copeland asked Thomas, too used to Laurel giving him a hard time to get worked up about it.

Thomas stared at the computer, scowling. He wanted to get home to Vi, but he just didn't like the idea of the postal inspector poking around at all, plus he had two hours to make up for. "She said she's going to have to take the evidence for her case. I don't like it."

"Well, she gave us time to do our tests, right?"

"Yeah."

"Relax then."

He knew he should.

But he couldn't.

Vi was humming when Thomas got home. She'd made a perhaps more elaborate than necessary dinner. It was the least she could do. Just like out at the ranch. If she could cook and clean up some, she didn't feel so bad for essentially sponging off people.

"Tata!" Mags squealed, getting up off the floor where she'd been happily playing with some magazines Vi had found in Thomas's office. They'd been in a recycling bin, so Vi didn't feel bad about letting Mags rip them apart.

She toddled over to Thomas, who picked her up on a big, dramatic swoop that made Magnolia squeal.

"I saw Franny outside. She told me to let you know she's heading home. At least I think that's what all those grunts meant."

Vi laughed. "Snooping around your house really got her creative juices flowing, and I don't think Mags's impressive concert of squeals was conducive for getting any of it written down."

He didn't look especially frustrated or tense, but he wasn't particularly happy either. Still, he came over, gave her a kiss, peered down at what she was making. "You didn't have to, but this looks amazing."

"I like to cook."

"Good, because I do not." He stood there, his arm around her while she stood over the stove. Mags sat on his hip, plucking at the chain around his neck that held his badge.

She waited for that to settle in her like a jolt. Fear. Worry. PTSD. Call it what you will. But he was holding her daughter, holding her. Everything he'd done for her, everything he'd been to her. It trumped that symbol of her old life. Her old mistakes.

She leaned into him, giving the pasta another stir. "What are you procrastinating telling me?"

He sighed, then kissed her hair. "That obvious, huh?"

"I'm learning to read the signs."

"A postal inspector came in today and had some questions about the envelope I received with the pictures. Something to do with mail fraud. She can't tell me how it connects quite yet, but I'm hoping to get more out of her tomorrow. She's probably going to give you a call. I imagine if she's staying here a few days, she'll want a face to face and to ask you questions."

"Can you be there?"

"She's very by the book, so I'm not sure she's going to go for that. That okay?"

She wanted to balk at that. At *all* of this. But she'd promised him. That she was ready. Ready to fight for herself and for Magnolia and a future with Thomas.

"Of course," she said firmly. "Whatever gets us to the end of this."

He settled Mags into her highchair, then said he wanted to take a quick shower. So she set the table and got Magnolia her dinner and let it cool a bit before Thomas came out and joined them.

They ate dinner and talked about different things. She knew he was carefully avoiding the topic of those pictures, and she let him. He patiently picked up Magnolia's sippy cup every time she gleefully tossed it to the ground.

"Where did you learn to be so good with kids?"

"I don't think I have any childless friends left. Except my Hart cousins, but that won't last forever and there's still kids running all over the place out at the ranch anyway. It's just…go to parties, see people, end up holding a baby or entertaining a toddler or feeding somebody, or be alone."

"You never did like to be alone."

"Not my forte. Though with as much work and social engagements I have these days, I don't mind a night home alone every once in a while. Well, as long as you're there." He grinned at her across the table.

And this domestic moment, that grin, his patience with her daughter maybe finally gave her the courage to ask a question that had been in the back of her mind since she'd seen him again.

"So, why didn't you ever get married?"

He shrugged. "Nothing stuck."

"Why? And *don't* say me. You haven't been pining after me for fifteen years."

"I guess not pining. You were always in the back of my mind, but you're right, it wasn't like I was expecting you to come back."

He didn't offer anything else. And maybe she should have let it go, but she…couldn't. "So?"

"I don't know. Nothing ever got serious."

"You are getting all the terrible nitty-gritty about my terrible relationship. The least you can do is tell me about your failures."

His mouth quirked at that. "I've got a demanding job, which isn't conducive to dating. If I ever got past the first few last-minute date cancellations, it is not my experience that women are particularly comfortable with me having a female partner, particularly one I think so highly of. That's mellowed out the past few years, what with Laurel's heap of kids and all and being out on maternity leave half the time. But it's been a sticking point."

Vi thought of the woman she'd met in his office yesterday. Pretty. Confident. In the same profession, so lots to talk about and lots of time spent together. "Was it ever fair to be a sticking point?"

His gaze went down to his plate. Then he took a very *large* bite of pasta. "This is delicious."

"Thomas."

"What? It *is* delicious." When she gave him a *look*, he sighed again. "Nothing ever happened with Laurel. Even before she got married what seems like a million years ago. And it never will. She's like a sister to me now."

"That is *not* what I asked."

"What did you ask?" he asked innocently. *Too* innocently. *"Thomas."*

"It was nothing."

"Oh. My. God." But she found herself laughing in spite of it, and that in itself was kind of amazing. Because she just…knew he loved her. In the here and now. He never made her question it, never used it like a weapon or an excuse. How could she sit here and pick that apart?

"It was a very brief crush when I first started at county," he said.

Of course, believing he loved *her* didn't mean she wasn't curious. "How brief?"

"I don't know. It was a long time ago. She met Grady not long after that, and then they just became…like my family. The whole lot of Carsons and Delaneys. Well, after Jen and I stopped dating anyway. Kinda swore off any Delaneys after that."

"Who's Jen?"

He reached down to pick up Magnolia's sippy cup. "Laurel's sister."

"You had a crush on Laurel and then dated her *sister*?"

"Very, very briefly. A long, *long* time ago." He got up,

took his empty plate to the sink. Then grabbed a washcloth and used it to clean up Magnolia while Vi watched him and finished her dinner.

Once Mags was clean, he took her now empty plate to the sink. Vi got up to put the leftovers away, trying to picture the Thomas she'd known. Skinny and baby-faced, becoming a cop, dating other women. Living a life, just like she had done.

And somehow they'd both ended up back here in Bent, in each other's lives. She didn't believe in fate anymore—no matter what he'd said at that party months ago about picking a dime up off the floor because of her.

Fate would have meant she'd been in an abusive marriage for years because it was meant to be.

No, there was no *fate*. There was only the choices you made.

She'd made some bad ones. Now she was making good ones.

"Are we done investigating my romantic history?" he asked, handing her a Tupperware so she could pack up the leftover pasta.

"I don't know. Maybe." She took it but faced him and trailed her fingers through his hair. "I snooped in your underwear drawer. Did you keep it the whole time? The picture."

"Not exactly, no. When my parents moved, they gave me a bunch of my high school stuff. I got rid of a lot of it. But I couldn't bring myself to get rid of that. I figured… No matter how it ended, it'd been a good four years. I learned a lot. Why not keep a memento?"

"Got any other mementos from other women who haven't stuck?"

He wrapped an arm around her, drew her close. "Not a

one." Then they both looked at Mags who'd pulled herself up on his pant leg and was tugging on his pants.

"She really loves you."

"Good, because I really love the both of you." He dropped a kiss on her mouth, then picked up Mags and pressed a kiss to her forehead.

They cleaned up the kitchen together. Put Mags to bed together. They fooled around on the couch, and for the first time in a very long time Vi really let herself relax. Enjoy.

Believe. That she was on the other side of *awful*.

So when the postal inspector called in the morning, she made an appointment to answer her questions at Thomas's house. Thomas insisted, since he had a doorbell camera and other security measures. They didn't have to tell the inspector Vi was living there just because they were meeting there.

Since Thomas had court, and so did Laurel, he'd offered Copeland to come over and sit with her, but Vi decided she'd rather do it alone.

She wanted to stand on her own two feet. For herself, as much as for Thomas.

When Thomas suggested he run Magnolia out to Audra at the ranch before work, so she could have full concentration to answer the inspector's questions and then have her tele-therapy appointment this afternoon without having to worry about Mags, she agreed.

"Use the security system. Mr. Marigold next door is always home and usually being nosy, so he'll let you know if anything is funny. Call me if you need anything. When Inspector Kay gets here, wait for me to text that it's really her at the doorbell camera, okay?"

Vi nodded, gave him a kiss, and then watched as he expertly wrangled Mags into her car seat. And she stood there, watching the car go, trying to fight that feeling this was all just too good to be true.

"I won't let it be," she muttered, turning back inside. She locked the front door and then took her time getting ready. Brushing her hair, putting on light makeup. Actually putting on jeans and a top instead of living in sweats and yoga pants.

When the knock sounded on the door, she waited for Thomas's text.

It's the postal inspector.

So she opened the door and smiled.

The woman held out a badge. "Hi, I'm Inspector Dianne Kay. Are you Vi Reynolds?"

Vi nodded. "Yes. Come on in."

The woman was pretty, polished. But she had that *cop* way of looking around, cataloging everything, and making Vi feel like she was a series of failures for them to judge.

Why didn't it feel like that when Thomas did the same thing, she wondered? Probably just knowing him.

They sat down at the kitchen table, and Inspector Kay took the offered coffee. "I just have a few questions about the envelope you received two days ago, and then I'll get out of your hair."

"Of course."

"You received an envelope, addressed to your name, at a ranch out in unincorporated Bent County?"

"Yes. That's where I've been living."

"And what were the contents of this envelope?"

"Don't you have the envelope?"

The inspector looked up from the notes she was taking. "I will once the Bent County detective bureau releases them to me. But I want to hear it, in your words. That will help my case."

"They were the same pictures that were in Detective Hart's envelope."

"Okay." The woman tapped her pen against the paper, studying Vi. "And you're the subject of the pictures that both you and Detective Hart received?"

"Yes."

"And in the pictures you received, you're injured as well?"

"Yes." She knew the woman wanted more information, but Vi knew enough about dealing with cops at this point. Postal inspector. Detective. SWAT. It didn't matter.

She wasn't giving up information she wasn't specifically asked for.

"Can you tell me the circumstances of those injuries?" Inspector Kay asked.

"How does that connect to mail fraud?"

"I don't know yet, and it might not." The inspector smiled kindly. "But I can't determine that if I don't know."

Vi inhaled and nodded. It made sense, even if she didn't like it. Still, she wasn't quite strong enough to meet the inspector's gaze. She looked down at her hands. "My ex-husband used to beat me."

"So, were these police report photos?" the inspector asked. She was being incredibly patient, but it didn't make Vi feel any better.

She clenched her hands into fists under the table and kept her voice even and calm. "No."

"Then…"

"A few of them I took myself, to document what he was doing to me." For as much as that had mattered. "He used to confiscate my phone all the time, so it's no surprise he has access to them. As for the ones I didn't take I wasn't aware he took those."

"And these pictures are from an incident how long ago?"

"I'm not sure. The ones I took were from about two years ago. The ones he took… I'd have to take some time and try to remember. We were married for almost five years."

"So, you…let him do this to you? For years? That's what you're saying."

Let him. Twin emotions assaulted her at that turn of phrase. A guilt and shame she was so familiar with, she almost sank into that. But there was a new feeling in there.

Outrage. Because her therapist, her cousins, her friends, Thomas, no one let her talk about herself that way.

So she wasn't about to let anyone else. "I was a victim of systematic physical, emotional and financial abuse, Inspector Kay."

The woman reached across the table, rested her hand over Vi's. "Of course you were. I wasn't trying to say otherwise. I'm just trying to get the facts."

"Those are the facts."

She nodded, but it gave Vi the same feeling as the cops she'd dealt with at Eric's precinct.

Like they just thought she was crazy. Or overdramatic.

"So, you think the sender was your ex-husband?" She flipped through her notebook. "Eric Carter?"

"Yes. I don't know who else would have access to those photographs."

"And do you have any idea of what connection your husband might have to the Plano Police Department return address he used?"

"Ex-husband."

"I'm sorry." And she sounded it. Her expression was

even a little chagrined. "Does your ex-husband have a connection to Plano that you know about?"

Vi had to stop being so touchy. "No. He was from Virginia. We lived in Richmond the entire time we were
married. As far as I know, almost all of his family are in
Virginia or Georgia. I suppose he could have a friend or
a former coworker who moved to Texas, but I don't know
of any specifically."

"Okay. That should be all the questions I have for
now. If you get any more suspicious mail—from Texas or
anywhere—would you contact me?" She pushed a business
card across the table. "Or if you think of any connection
Eric Carter might have or have had with Texas?"

Vi nodded, relieved this was over. The inspector stood
and Vi led her back to the front door, opened it for her.

The inspector paused, looked her over once, that cop cal-
culation not well hidden. But then she smiled. "Don't worry,
ma'am. We're going to get to the bottom of this. I promise."

Vi wished it made her feel better.

Chapter Nine

"Well, that was a waste of time," Laurel grumbled as they stepped out of the courthouse together.

So often trips to court were. It seemed more often than not the defendant wasn't too keen on showing up to their own trial. Or their lawyer got things stalled out for another month.

He'd pulled his phone out of his pocket the minute they were released. He had a text from Vi.

She just left. Run-of-the mill questions. Hope court went well.

"Everything good?" Laurel asked, sliding into the passenger seat since he'd driven them over.

"Vi said the questions were pretty run-of-the-mill."

"You're going to have to surrender those envelopes and pictures today."

"I know." He blew out a long breath. "Want to take a long, *long* lunch?"

"It won't change anything."

"No, it won't," Thomas muttered. They hadn't gotten any prints off the envelope. Nothing that could give them proof on who'd sent it. Still, it grated. He didn't want to surrender evidence that had been sent to him to some federal agency.

"So, what's your theory? Coincidence, or this Eric guy is up to more bad than just terrorizing his ex-wife?"

He knew what Laurel was doing. She was posing it as a question, but she was reminding him there was more to this case then just those pictures. Because of course it wasn't coincidence. The postal inspector's case was bigger than whatever Vi's ex was up to.

Even if to *him*, and to Vi, the biggest thing was Eric causing her harm.

"I bet that postal inspector would let you in on more of her case if you took her out to dinner."

He eyed Laurel out of the corner of his eye as he drove. "And if you were to take out a male postal inspector to get more details on a case, how would Grady react?"

Laurel laughed. And then she laughed harder. "Touché." They reached the parking lot of the station and got out.

"You bringing her to Cam and Hilly's baby shower this weekend?" Laurel asked as they grabbed their bags out of the back.

"Trying to convince her. She acted a little squirrelly about it."

"Guess she's got a reason."

Thomas frowned, because he didn't know what that reason would be.

Laurel nudged him as they walked through the parking lot. "Now who's acting squirrelly?"

"Not squirrelly. I just don't…get it. But I haven't had time to think about it. I have to know they're safe before I can worry about little dumb stuff." Dumb stuff like why she didn't want to be in his life outside of the small worlds they'd created.

So maybe that was the answer. Laurel's *guess she's got a reason.*

Vi still didn't trust those worlds outside the ones she'd built. And could he really blame her after what she'd endured?

"You know, I hope this one sticks," Laurel said as he gestured her to go inside ahead of him.

"Yeah, me too. Why?"

"You deserve a nice family, Hart."

He liked to think so, but he also knew... For the past fifteen years, maybe nothing romantic had worked out, but that didn't mean he'd been alone. "Got one, don't I?"

She smiled at him. "Yeah, you do. But more doesn't hurt."

When they walked into their office, the postal inspector was already there. She was sitting in a chair and looking at her phone and took her time addressing them.

"Got a few minutes for me, Detective Hart?"

"Sure thing."

She paused, as if waiting for Laurel to give them privacy. Laurel, bless her, pretended like she didn't notice and went over to their desk and settled herself into the chair, then busied herself with the computer.

Thomas had to fight back a smile.

"I talked to Eric Carter this morning. He says he doesn't know anything about any envelopes or Texas."

"Naturally."

"I also spoke with a few of the people he works with, including his captain. No one knew of any connections he might have to Texas. He hasn't missed a scheduled day of work in months *and* hasn't taken any time off."

"Are you going to investigate that further? Someone can get from Richmond to Texas on a weekend off."

She lifted a shoulder. "Look, I can't rule him out, but I can't concentrate on him without more of a lead. There's no evidence he's left Virginia, and the postal stamp *is* from Texas. It's feeling a little bit more like a dead end than a lead."

"So how do you explain the fact he's the only one who would have had those photos?"

The inspector sighed. "I don't know, Detective Hart. I'd like to. Part of that will be continuing my investigation by focusing on the evidence we *do* have. I'd like the envelopes and their contents." She smiled, but there was no confusing that smile for anything but politeness over a demand. "Now."

Laurel stood. "Why don't I go get them for you?" she offered.

Thomas nodded, even though he hated it. He wasn't getting around a federal agency on this. Besides, he had copies. It wasn't a total loss. Laurel gave his arm a reassuring squeeze before she left the office.

Once Laurel was gone, the inspector spoke again. "Can I ask why I questioned someone at a house that you own, Detective Hart?"

Whatever accusations Inspector Kay was offering were veiled under a smile and a friendly enough delivery. Thomas tried to match it instead of getting defensive. He hadn't expected her to check on the owner of the house.

"Like I said yesterday, she's a friend." Thomas kept himself as relaxed as possible. "She lives with family and she didn't want them worried, so I let her use my place. Is that a problem?"

"No, I just want to make sure I know all the details of the case."

"It's a small town, ma'am. We watch out for each other around here. You've got all the details."

"I'm heading back to Denver this afternoon, but it's possible I'll be back." She stood up from the chair. Just a *shade* too close. But he pretended not to notice.

"You've got my number. Feel free to call me if something changes."

He smiled thinly. "I will. I hope you'll do the courtesy of letting me know when you wrap up this case."

"Of course."

She stayed there a beat, and then Laurel came in. She slid a sealed evidence envelope between what little space Inspector Kay had left between her and him.

"Here you go," she said cheerfully.

The inspector took them. "I'm not your enemy, guys. I hope you realize that." Then she scooted past him, *against* him, and out the door.

"She's right," Thomas muttered in frustration, irritation. He might not like her on a personal level, but it wasn't like they were on opposite sides. They were both looking for the truth. He just had a vested personal connection. "We're all on the same side. I've got to stop acting like I'm the only one who can protect Vi."

Laurel patted him on the back. "You're doing all right, Hart. We'll get there."

He wished he believed it.

VI THOUGHT HER therapy session went well enough. She talked about the postal inspector's questions, and the comment about *letting* Eric happen.

She worked through her feelings on that, why she might be touchy about word choice, and how some people projected their own issues onto others. Whatever the inspector thought didn't have anything to do with Vi.

So she had to let it go.

Easier said than done, but at least she had an action plan. When Thomas got home, Mags in tow, her heart filled.

Who else's opinion could matter when she had these two?

But that joy quickly petered out when they sat down to dinner, and Thomas started talking about *socializing*.

"The baby shower is Saturday at noon. Kids welcome. It's basically just a barbecue and we're all bringing baby gifts. You know, Hilly is a nurse. Just started last year. She could give you information if you were still looking in that direction."

"Thomas, I don't know that Mags and I should go."

He didn't say anything at first. There was a kind of heavy silence that might have reminded her of her past if it wasn't *Thomas* sitting there.

"Okay." He took the last bite of food from his plate, put it in his mouth, then got up and moved to the sink. Without anything else.

Vi looked helplessly at Mags, who'd made a mess of herself as usual. And like he often did, Thomas came over with a washcloth and wiped her up.

But he didn't say anything, and he didn't smile. And it made her feel…small. Like her stomach was tied in a million knots. She couldn't finish her meal.

"Thomas. Talk to me."

"About what?" He went over to the sink, dropped the washcloth in it. Turned on the sink.

She got up, frustration and some other emotion she didn't quite understand brewing deep inside her. "You can't be afraid to tell me what you want just because I have this… trauma sitting there. This won't work if you treat me with kid gloves."

"I did tell you what I wanted. You said no, and I said okay."

"And now you're mad."

He shook his head, and to his credit, he didn't actually seem *mad*. He turned off the sink, turned to her. "I'm not mad. I'm...confused and disappointed."

"But you said okay."

"What am I supposed to say?"

"That you're confused and disappointed."

"I'm not going to manipulate you into going to this with me. If you don't want to, that's your choice. And I'll live with it. The end."

"It's not the end, because it's not...*manipulating* to explain to me how you feel about something I've done."

He crossed his arms over his chest. There *was* some anger, but it was carefully guarded. "What about *your* feelings? What about *your* decision? You want me to unload, but you won't even tell me why you won't go."

"I just..." Maybe it was because she'd had her therapy session this afternoon that she found the courage to say it. "I hate the idea anyone I meet has to eventually know the truth about me. They'll know what happened to me and it colors who I am."

He didn't say anything to that, didn't drop his arms, but that carefully guarded anger turned into something else. Something too close to pity for her liking.

"It doesn't color who you are to me."

"I know. But that postal inspector..."

Thomas stiffened. "What about her?"

Vi shrugged. She didn't have the words for it. "I don't know. I don't like the way she talked to me. The questions she had to ask. I know that's not fair, but it just... I'm tired of having to dredge it all back up. When I was living at the ranch, I only talked to Audra, Rosalie and Franny. I barely left. I felt…safe."

He inhaled. "Do you feel safe here, Vi?"

She didn't even have to think about the answer. "I do."

"All right then."

Mags chose that moment to throw her sippy cup halfway across the room, knocking over Vi's half-full glass of milk. They all jumped to action to clean everything up, and then comfort Mags when she started crying.

They put Mags to bed. They didn't make out on the couch. Maybe they'd both had a rough enough day. But when they crawled into bed, he pulled her against him and held her close and tight.

"I love you, Vi."

"I love you too." And she fell asleep fast enough, or must have, because the next thing she knew a trilling phone woke her up. Panic immediately slammed through her.

Eric was calling.

Eric…

"Hello," Thomas's deep voice said into the quiet room.

For a moment, addled by sleep, she thought he'd answered her phone. But her hand was on her phone on the nightstand. And the screen was black. No call coming through.

It had been *his* phone ringing.

"And it can't wait until morning?" he said in low tones as Mags made some whimpering noises.

He grunted some kind of assent, then put his phone down on the nightstand again. "I've got to get down to the station," he whispered. "A break on an old case we can't wait on." He pushed out of the bed. He was only a shadow in the dark. Then he cursed. "Hell, Vi. I can't leave you here alone."

"It's okay," she said, her mind whirling a bit. Still hung up on Eric. Weird threatening calls from robotic voices were usually the only phone calls that woke her up in the middle of the night.

He slid out of the room, and she could see the light come on under the crack of the door. Mags had fussed, but had quieted back down, so Vi snuck out of the room, letting in the least amount of light.

He'd brought his clothes out here and was putting them on. "I'm sorry." And he looked genuinely worried, genuinely conflicted as he pulled on his county polo. "I don't usually get called in in the middle of the night, but I should have thought this possibility through when I had you guys come stay here."

"We'll be all right. You said it yourself, the postal inspector talked to Eric at work today. In Virginia. He's just trying to scare me. Not hurt me. You can't watch me 24/7, Thomas. It's just not possible."

"I'm going to see if I can get a deputy to drive by, maybe park outside for a bit." He strode over to the closet. She usually didn't watch him do this part, because she hated knowing there was a gun in the house.

But tonight, she did. Watched him reach up to the gun safe on the top shelf in the closet, unlock it with the key on his keychain, and then pull out the gun and shove it into the holster attached to his belt.

As their marriage had gone on, seeing Eric in his uniform, with his guns, had made her more and more nervous. Always wondering when he'd turn it on her.

But tonight, she worried about what Thomas might have to face that would force him to pull his gun. Because that was the only way she knew he'd use it.

He crossed back to her, pressed a kiss to her mouth. "All

the back doors are locked. Just make sure the security is all set up once I lock the front door behind me. Okay?"

"I'll be okay. We'll be okay. I promise." She managed a smile.

He definitely didn't smile back. He was going off to do dangerous work in the middle of the night. That was his job. A job she was very familiar with, because Eric had done the same.

Of course, even in the beginning of their relationship, before he'd started hitting her, she'd never minded. It had always been nice to get a little time alone. And he usually came back from an actual emergency call in a good mood.

Work made him feel important, powerful. It was when he felt weak, small and useless that he took to using his fists to make her feel the same.

Thomas stepped out the door and closed it behind him. She heard him lock it with his key. Then she made sure the security system was on.

She didn't think she'd be going back to sleep, so she settled herself on the couch and turned on the TV. She must have dozed off eventually, though, because she was jerked awake by the text message notification on her phone.

She looked at the screen, thinking the text would be from Thomas. But it was from an unknown number instead.

Count your days.

Chapter Ten

Thomas arrived at the station and found Copeland in their office. His expression was grim, but there was a light in his eyes. Because after months of nothing, and just having to *accept* that they couldn't prove Allen Scott had killed his wife, they had a glimmer of hope.

A woman was accusing Scott of battery.

It wasn't his poor dead wife, whose death had been ruled a suicide, but it was something. A chance to dig deeper once again. And Scott behind bars, as long as their victim didn't bolt.

"Deputy Clarion's with the victim at the hospital. Scott's in holding. Which one you want?"

Thomas considered either option. It all felt a little too... *close* now. Like he'd see Vi in the victim, and her ex-husband in the assaulter. He didn't like either eventuality, but he knew which one would allow him to be at least somewhat in control. "Probably best if I handle the victim."

Copeland nodded, and then got him up to speed on the police report from the deputies. They had a quick discussion about strategy, about what questions they wanted asked of both parties, and what steps they'd take after questioning.

"You going to be okay with this?" Copeland asked, eyeing Thomas like he didn't quite trust him, right before they split up.

"It's not the case." Or at least it wasn't *only* the case. "I don't like leaving Vi alone with all her stuff going on. I've got the night shift driving by the house every once in a while, but with Clarion at the hospital, they're short-staffed."

"But this can't wait," Copeland said.

"No, it can't. Which is why I'm here."

Copeland nodded as if that was good enough for him, and then they split up. Thomas drove to the hospital armed with the police report the deputies had taken, additional information from Copeland, and the usual mix of dread and anticipation.

He would not like the answers he got tonight, but answers would lead to justice. Justice for a woman like Vi, and a woman who hadn't been lucky enough to survive an awful man.

Deputy Clarion stood outside the victim's hospital room. They exchanged greetings.

"Was it your call?" Thomas asked.

Clarion nodded. "Neighbor called it in. Scott was gone by the time we got there, and she was in rough shape, but she named Scott. Gave us his address and everything."

"Good." There was more he wanted to say, like *Let's get this SOB*, but with Clarion's body cam no doubt rolling, Thomas kept it to himself.

When he entered the hospital room, after he knocked and the victim gave him the go-ahead, Christine Smith looked at him through a swollen eye. She sat in a hospital bed, her face an array of stitches, bandages and loud bruises. She had one arm in a cast, and thanks to the doctor's report, he knew she had three cracked ribs, a bruised kidney and a fractured ankle.

"Ma'am. My name is Detective Thomas Hart, and I'd like to ask you a few questions about what happened tonight, if you're up for it." She'd told the doctor and the deputy she was, but Thomas wanted to make sure.

"I've answered a lot of questions already," she said. But she clasped her hands in her lap and didn't send him away.

"I know, and I know how frustrating that can be."

"What about traumatizing?" she demanded with a snap.

"That too," he agreed, and tried not to think of what Vi would have gone through. Answering these questions, only to have the interviewer not believe her. Only to have every *right* step thwarted, all because her ex had worn a badge.

"But you still have to ask them," the woman said on a long sigh.

"I'm afraid so. And I'd like to record your answers, if you're okay with that."

She looked away from him, at the window. The curtains were closed, so it wasn't like there was anything to see beyond, but she still stared. He gave her time. Time to breathe. Time to think.

Eventually, and gingerly, she nodded. "Yeah. Whatever will end this."

He set up the recorder, then asked her about the evening, and she answered questions in surprising detail. There was a kind of determined detachment as she described how the man she'd been dating had started to beat her in a furious rage.

She didn't shed any tears, until she got to the last part. "All I did was ask about his wife. And he just…lost it. He wanted to kill me. And I still don't know *why*."

Thomas's heart beat triple time, but he kept his voice even. His eyes steady. "Does Scott have a wife?"

"She died. And he'd mentioned it, played up the grieving widower thing." Christine swallowed. "So a few times I've asked what happened, thinking that's kind of what he wanted. To talk about it, you know?"

Thomas nodded.

"But tonight, the story didn't match what he'd told me a few dates ago. I pointed that out. I haven't had much luck with guys, so maybe I was kind of a bitch about it."

"Doesn't mean he gets to hit you, Ms. Smith."

She inhaled sharply, then winced a little. "No, it doesn't. Anyway, I was getting on him for lying to me and he just… snapped. Said he was going to kill me."

"He said that to you? In those words?"

She looked Thomas dead in the eye. Tears glimmered there, but she didn't blink, didn't look away. "He told me in those words. He told me he was going to kill me, just like he killed his wife."

For a moment, Thomas didn't say anything. He had to fight his reaction. It wasn't enough to charge Allen with murder, but it was a step toward this being a lot more than just a domestic assault case.

"Are you willing to say all this in front of a jury?"

Her jaw worked for a second, and she was clearly in pain, even if she was on some pain medication, but when she spoke, it was with conviction.

"I'm willing to scream it from the rooftops," she said firmly, her expression grim, despite the bruises, bandages and swelling. "I want him to rot in hell."

So do I.

Vi HAD THOUGHT about waiting. She'd thought about trying to wave down the cop Thomas had driving by the house intermittently.

But in the end, she'd called Laurel Delaney-Carson. If

only because Rosalie was too far away. It felt safer, smarter, to call someone she knew lived close by. Someone Thomas trusted more than anyone else. Someone he'd told her to call if there was trouble.

She was considering it a leap of faith. A gesture to Thomas that…she was here to stay and fight for their lives together, even if sometimes she wanted to stay hidden away forever.

God, she hoped it was the right choice.

She opened the front door, because Laurel had called and told her she was there. The woman stepped inside, closed and locked the door behind her in quick, efficient *cop* moves. She was dressed in the same kind of drab uniform Thomas usually wore—khakis, a Bent County Sheriff's Department polo. Her hair was pulled back in a tight ponytail, and even though it was the middle of the night, she looked ready to handle anything that came her way.

Vi had to swallow down the battalion of nerves duking it out in her throat. She was in pajamas. Her hair was probably insane right now. She should have thought about her appearance, but she hadn't wanted to wake up Magnolia and…

This wasn't a *social* call. Vi breathed out. It didn't matter how she looked. It mattered that she'd received a threatening text message in the middle of the night, after Thomas had been called in to work.

When she'd called Laurel, Laurel had assured her that Thomas was fine. At the local hospital questioning a victim. So, it hadn't been some fake call. Thomas was okay.

And Vi was okay too. Maybe the text was more threatening than the usual screeds about how useless and terrible she was, and even more threatening than the voicemail he'd left a few months ago saying he couldn't wait until she was a rotting corpse. Because that had been disturbing, but vague enough.

Count your days wasn't vague. It was a countdown.

Vi let out a slow breath to steady herself. She'd done the right thing. This woman was Thomas's friend, his mentor. Even if Laurel didn't believe *Vi*, she'd at least do her due diligence for Thomas.

Unless she convinces him you're just as crazy as Eric always said.

The fear of that, no matter how hard she tried to push it away, made her stutter when she spoke. "Thank you for coming. I shouldn't have bothered you in the middle of the night. I know you've got kids and…"

"It's part of the job," Laurel said gently. "If it wasn't, Thomas would be here and handling this himself, right?"

Vi nodded. She was almost glad he wasn't. She wasn't sure what he would have done if *that* had been the message that had woken them up. She was half-afraid he would have flown to Virginia himself.

It seemed better, or at least *almost* better, to deal with someone who might not believe her.

"Besides," Laurel continued. "My husband is used to middle-of-the-night phone calls and me being called away. He's superdad at that. We've been doing this for a long time. So, don't worry about anything. You did the exact right thing. Now, can I see the text message?"

Vi nodded and pulled her phone out of her pocket. She'd had to unlock her phone to call Laurel, but she'd left the text message unread. After a short hesitation, she forced herself to open the message and hold the phone out to Laurel.

Laurel took the phone, read the screen. Her expression didn't change, except maybe her mouth got a little tighter. "Not particularly clever."

"No, not his strong suit."

She looked up at Vi. "You're sure it's your ex-husband, then?"

Vi wanted to look away. To shrug and say who really knew anything. But if Laurel told Thomas she acted that way… "I don't know who else it could be but proving it is the problem."

Laurel nodded. "No, it's not going to be easy to prove, but that doesn't mean we won't give it our best shot. We'll try to get some information on the number, to start. I want you to screenshot that message, text it to me. I'll forward it to Thomas after he's done with his current case, or you can. I know he's got a file of these from when we first got those pictures."

Vi nodded, but she didn't act right away. Maybe Thomas hadn't told Laurel everything. Maybe Laurel didn't fully understand. Even if she used *we* like they were all in this together.

She forced herself to screenshot it, forward it to Laurel's number. She'd forward it to Rosalie in the morning too.

"I'll have Thomas call the postal inspector. Maybe something about this can connect everything."

Vi tried not to pull a face. She just *hated* all this being passed around, but it had to be. It *had* to be.

Laurel didn't ask too many questions. At first Vi was relieved, but she got more and more tense about it as she started to realize it was because there was already a file. All about her and her ex-husband. Because of the pictures. Because of the postal inspector. Because of…

She stopped the negative thought spiral. Any *becauses* were due to *Eric*. And she had to remember that.

But Eric was still the crux of the problem.

"The thing is, even if you connect it to Eric, it doesn't

matter. He has his whole precinct under his thumb. He's so great, so brave, his ex-wife must just be crazy. He even got his lawyer to somehow make it look like *he* filed for divorce and *I* contested it."

Laurel was quiet for a moment, nodding slowly. "All of that may be true, but if he's mixed up in this federal case about mail fraud, he's crossing lines no amount of influence can fix for him."

"Are you sure about that?" Vi asked, not certain how that question sounded to Laurel. Because to *her* ears it felt as derisive and scoffing as she felt. Which wasn't the right attitude, she knew.

But it had been *years*. Why should she believe something could change?

Because you're here. Alive and happy. In love with a great guy who's protecting you.

As it so often did, that truth and hope felt too dangerous to believe in.

Laurel studied her, like she didn't quite understand the question. "I know justice doesn't always work out, but—"

"There's no buts to that. Sometimes, no amount of doing the right thing gets anyone justice. I did everything you're supposed to. Maybe not right away. Maybe I didn't get out when I should have, but when the abuse got to a certain point, I called the cops. I wanted to press charges. He made me out to be the villain, and *nothing* ever stuck to him. I know what cops can do."

Laurel didn't say anything right away. She didn't even look mad or pitying. There was a kind of resigned sadness to her sigh. "Fair enough. Are you worried that Thomas would do the same thing?"

For a moment, just a moment, it seemed her whole world tilted. The idea of Thomas shaping everyone's thoughts and feelings about her. That all this would just disappear, and everyone would think of her as Eric had portrayed her.

But even as the picture took shape in her imagination, she couldn't imagine Thomas doing any of it. It was still just Eric, poisoning her life here.

Because she knew better than to believe in someone wholeheartedly. She knew better than to think happily-ever-afters were real or easy. But she also knew Thomas Hart.

"No. I know he wouldn't. I just…"

"Good. I'm glad to hear it," Laurel said firmly. "Now, I don't expect you to trust the rest of us point-blank, but Thomas has been a friend of mine for well over a decade. He's my daughter Sunny's godfather. He's a great cop and a greater guy."

Vi knew all this.

"I have *never* seen him so happy as he's been the past few months. Or so protective of…anyone, and he's a pretty protective guy. He talks about your daughter like she hung the moon."

And even though Vi *knew* that last little bit, it still had tears welling in her eyes.

"I can't pretend to know what it's like to be victimized by your own husband, but…there are people in my life who I loved, who turned out to be the opposite of what I thought they were, and I know what that does. It makes it hard to trust people."

"I trust Thomas."

"Good. And I hope somewhere along the line, you learn you can trust the rest of us too. Anyone who's got Thomas's back, has yours. I can promise you that. He'll call me a busybody, but oh well. Maybe I'll just accept I am one. If you let all of us get to know you, the way Thomas would like us to, then we'd all have your backs because of *you*, not just Thomas. It's just what we do."

Vi realized this wasn't about the case so much anymore. "He told you I don't want to come to the baby shower."

"It's my brother's baby shower," Laurel said, a bit ruefully. "So, it's not like he was spilling state secrets. It was more an RSVP conversation thing. And, because I'm an *excellent* detective, I deduced that wasn't exactly his preference."

"No. It wasn't. But it's…a private matter."

Laurel's rueful smile didn't change. She didn't get offended, or at least she didn't show it if she did. She looked down at her phone. "Thomas is almost here, so I'll get out of your hair and let you guys talk. You're probably exhausted."

Which was when Vi realized Laurel hadn't brought that up just because she'd seen the opportunity. Or at least, not only. Laurel had brought it up to spend more time here. Time until Thomas got back.

Something about that had Vi saying something more vulnerable than she liked to get with veritable strangers. But, she supposed, if she loved Thomas she had to stop letting everyone he cared about be a stranger.

"It's hard. To…let people get to know you when you're still learning not to hate yourself."

Laurel took a deep, careful breath. Her smile was kind, but a little sad. "Fair enough, Vi. Fair enough."

Chapter Eleven

"It's okay."

Vi said that before Thomas had even managed to get his arms around her. But he hugged her close anyway. Tight, just to assure himself she was here, good, in one piece.

Laurel's voicemail had explained the situation and assured him everything was fine, but that didn't mean he'd been fully able to believe it.

"I don't like the timing, Vi," he muttered into her hair. Finally able to breathe again. Maybe because he'd spent his night talking to a woman who'd been beaten so badly, he just...wasn't okay.

"No, I don't either," she said, patting his back. "But it's not like he could have set up you getting called away. I think it's just a coincidence."

Thomas nodded. He finally released her, at least a little. Looked back at Laurel. "Thanks for coming."

"No thanks needed. You know that. I've got the text. I'll add it to our file, write the report. I was thinking we should pass it along to the postal inspector too, just in case it might connect to something."

Thomas nodded. "Yeah, good idea."

"I'm going to head into the station, do all that. You get some rest. We'll talk more later."

Thomas nodded. He couldn't bear to let Vi go, and he knew Laurel would give him a hard time if he said thanks again. "I'll be back in around noon. Copeland and I have a meeting with the prosecutor."

"Get some sleep in the meantime, huh?" Laurel said, then let herself out.

Thomas hugged Vi close again. He wasn't sure he'd taken a full breath from the time he listened to Laurel's voicemail until now. "I want to see the message."

He felt Vi stiffen. "Okay, but…"

He pulled back so he could read her expression. And too easily he could see those pictures. See the woman in the hospital bed as her instead of his current victim. "But what?"

She studied his face. "I just don't want you to… Well, I guess it's stupid to say I don't want you to worry."

"Maybe not stupid, but pointless."

She sighed, then nodded. She pulled her phone out, hit a few buttons and handed it to him. He read the screen.

Count your days.

He didn't lose it. God, he wanted to, but there was a sleeping baby and victimized woman in his house. "That's far more of a concrete threat than the others have been."

Vi nodded. "I know."

Before he could think of anything else to say, he heard Mags start to make noises from his room. Vi moved first, but Thomas stopped her.

"I got her."

"You've been up all night."

"So have you."

"Yes, but just sitting around. You've been working. Is everything…okay?"

Thomas almost nodded, but it wasn't really *okay*. "A woman came in, badly beaten. She ID'd the guy who did it to her, as a man Copeland and I investigated a few months ago for murder. We couldn't find enough evidence, and the death was ruled a suicide. So, this has two parts to it. We've got him on the assault, now we want to try to get him on that murder."

"Who did he kill?" she asked, like she knew.

Thomas didn't have to tell her. He could lie. He could do a lot of things, but he held her gaze. "His wife."

Vi nodded once, sharply. "Well, then I'm glad he's in jail."

"We're going to do everything we can to make sure it stays that way." He stepped into the room where Mags was fussing. She'd pulled herself up on the rail of the crib. But when she saw him, she stopped whimpering and grinned.

It eased so much of what had felt like barbed wire wrapped around his lungs. This sweet little baby, who loved him easily and without reservation, just because he'd shown up in her life.

All because Vi had been strong enough to escape an impossible situation, and she'd had enough family to help see her through. It wasn't lost on him how lucky they all were, even in the midst of what felt like a decided lack of luck.

He picked up Mags, who sleepily snuggled into his shoulder. She'd be running around like a screeching banshee in about fifteen minutes, but the first time when she woke up, she was sweet and sleepy and cuddly.

Thomas let that soothe him. Or he tried to.

Eric Carter was going to come after Vi. He had no doubts about that. And with the text message, Thomas knew that was coming sooner rather than later.

So, he'd have to do everything to protect her and Mags.

But not just physically. After tonight at the hospital, he needed Vi to understand. Not just because he was here, but because he said the words.

"I need you to know, I see this a lot. Before you came. I'm sure I'll see it more. And I may not be in that victim's seat, but I know just how much strength and courage it takes to stand up against someone who could do that to you. I know that everyone thinks it's easy because you're hurt and angry. And I know they're wrong, because anyone who would physically hurt someone is taking something away from them. Nothing about surviving this is easy, and even if I've never experienced that, I do understand it."

She kept very still. Her expression was almost startled. Before she blew out a breath.

"Then I need you to know that I called Laurel because I knew it was what you wanted. And no matter what happens because of Eric, I don't want to hurt you, Thomas."

He held out his arm, and she stepped into him. One arm holding Mags against him, one arm curled around Vi's shoulder. A trio.

A family.

He kissed her hair. "I love you, Vi."

"I love you too. And I'll...go to the baby shower."

He tried to follow her. For a moment, he didn't even know what baby shower she meant. "Oh. Well, we don't have to talk about that right now, sweetheart. I just..."

"No, I want to go. I want you to know that I want to go." She swallowed, tears swimming in her blue eyes. She swallowed audibly. "I *want* to be part of your life, Thomas."

THOMAS HAD TO go into the station for a few hours the morning of the baby shower, so Vi drove with Mags out to the ranch to catch up with everyone, and to see if Audra had any clothes suitable for a baby shower she could borrow.

Thomas had been a little...overprotective the past few days. Rightfully so, she knew. And maybe it could be frustrating not to be able to go do what she wanted, whenever she wanted. But she also didn't want to do anything that would put her or Mags in danger.

So every day was carefully planned. Monitored. When she reached the ranch, she texted Thomas that she'd arrived. Then she tried to put the worry aside and focus on an outfit for a baby shower.

Audra took her through her closet since she was the closest in size to Vi, and it was a blessed slice of normal. To try on outfits, have a trio of women weigh in on which one was the best.

In the end, she picked a cute floral skirt and her own plain T-shirt, with some of Franny's jewelry. She felt cute and casual and...well, *nervous.*

She didn't regret saying she'd go. She couldn't. It was a symbol. It was giving Thomas something when he'd already given her *so much*. It was important, and she supposed that was why she was so nervous.

This wasn't just a baby shower. It was a gesture, and she desperately wanted it to go well. She was studying herself in the mirror, Mags playing with Franny and Rosalie on Franny's bedroom floor when her phone rang.

She grabbed it, looked at the caller and tried not to blanch.

Franny must have seen it, because she got to her feet. "Vi—"

"It's the postal inspector's number." Vi tried to smile, because hey, it wasn't *Eric*. But it was probably about him.

She answered the phone, stepped out of the room, knowing everyone would look after Mags.

"Hello?"

"Hi, Ms. Reynolds. This is Postal Inspector Kay. How are you?"

"I'm…fine."

"And no doubt stressed that I called you," she replied, good-naturedly. "But I have good news. I'm really close to being able to put out a warrant for Eric Carter's arrest. But I have a few follow-up questions I'd like to ask you. Are you home?"

Vi thought her knees might have dissolved. She had to lean against the wall to stay upright. "Arrest?"

"Yes. Tampering with mail is a federal offense, hence my involvement with all this. As long as my case is airtight, he's going to do some time. So, are you home?"

"Uh, no," Vi said, her mind whirling. Federal offense. Arrest. Eric. Was this *real*? "Well, yes." Because the inspector didn't know she actually lived with Thomas. "Not where we talked initially. I'm at my cousin's ranch out by Sunrise. It's a ways from Bent," she tacked on, remembering the inspector wasn't from around here.

"I'm not too far from there. There's a coffee place just off the highway, isn't there?"

"Yes. Coffee Klatsch."

"Okay, can I meet you there in fifteen minutes or so? I just have a few questions. Won't take more than a half hour."

Vi thought about the timing. She still had two hours before the baby shower. She could do this, get it over with, and maybe know more about the actual potential of Eric being arrested. "Okay, I can do that."

"Great. See you soon."

They hung up and Vi returned to the room. Everyone looked up at her with questions in their eyes. Vi wasn't sure she had any answers. Her brain couldn't really function beyond *arrest.*

But the inspector needed some answers first. "Can you guys watch Mags while I run an errand?"

"What kind of errand?" Rosalie demanded.

"I just have to meet with the postal inspector. Answer a few more questions. Real quick at Coffee Klatsch."

"Let me come with you," Rosalie said, getting to her feet. "I have some questions for *her.*"

Vi considered it. She knew Rosalie was running her own investigation. She also knew Rosalie didn't always know when to be…polite.

"I think it's best if I do this alone. She said it'll only take a half hour at most. Guys, she said she's *this* close to putting out an arrest warrant for Eric."

Rosalie and Franny exchanged a look.

"I don't want to get my hopes up, but this is huge. It's just a few questions, then I'll be back by noon to pick up Mags and head out to the baby shower. And I'll text Thomas where I'm going too."

She went over to Mags, kissed her head. "I'll be back before you guys know it." Then she hurried out before Rosalie could decide she needed to come anywhere. On her way to her car, she wrote out the text to Thomas.

Meeting the postal inspector at Coffee Klatsch to answer some questions.

Thought she'd headed back to Denver.

Apparently not.

Take Rosalie with you.

I'd like to stay in the inspector's good graces. It's just a short drive there and back to the ranch. I'll keep updating.

Okay. Love you.

She texted back her own Love you, then drove out to the coffee house. The postal inspector was already there, leaning against the trunk of her rental car.

Vi pulled into the parking space right next to her, then steeled herself to face the intimidating postal inspector.

Who thought Eric had committed a *federal offense*. That was enough to get Vi out of the car.

"Don't you look pretty." Inspector Kay said in greeting. She shaded her eyes against the sun.

Vi managed a smile, doing the same. "Oh, well, thanks. I'm going to a baby shower."

She frowned for a split second, but then smiled kindly. "Why didn't you say so? These questions can wait. I don't want to make you late."

"No, you said it'd be quick. Let's just get it over with."

The inspector seemed to think this over. "All right. Well, let's skip coffee then," she said, waving at the building. "When you received the envelope, the address was your cousin's ranch."

Which wasn't a new question at *all*. "Yes."

"I talked to the mail carrier, and he said he didn't think he'd seen an envelope that fit the description that day. Thought he would have remembered that since he's been delivering mail to the Young Ranch for years."

"Well, it was in the mailbox with the rest of the mail. Thomas asked Audra about it, and that's what she said."

"Yes, that's all in the report. It's just strange, because the mailman who delivered the envelope to the police station remembered dropping it off there *and* is on security footage doing so. He's also been with the USPS for a few years, so unlikely involved."

This all felt like the very *opposite* of leads that would end in Eric being arrested.

"Does your ex-husband have any connection to Bent County? And listen, I know you've probably already thought of that, but I just want to make sure there's no tiny stone you've left unturned."

The thought absolutely *petrified* her. But she tried to think through that. Tried to focus on what the inspector was asking. "I thought long and hard before I came here last year," Vi said carefully. "If I'd thought he had even a tiny connection to Bent County, I wouldn't have ended up here."

"What about to the post office in some way? A friend who was a mailman? A case maybe he talked about with postal inspection?"

"There was a case where he worked with a postal inspector," Vi said. She only remembered because before that she hadn't even known postal inspectors were a thing. And Eric talked about what a joke of a job it was, and how useless he'd thought the guy working with him on the case was. "I don't remember details, but I know it was a long time ago. Early on in our marriage."

The inspector nodded and typed something into her phone. "That's good. Maybe I can get a subpoena for that information. It's something to go on, anyway."

"Really?"

She nodded. "Really. We're so close. We just need one little break. One little connection, and the dominoes will start to fall. I'm sure of it."

Vi stood there, the wind blowing around them. She was dressed for a baby shower, going to meet a bunch of her boyfriend's friends and be folded into yet another area of his life.

And this might be over.

"I might have a few more for you once I get a chance to question him myself," Inspector Kay said. "I'm hoping to do that Monday afternoon. Will you be around Tuesday morning? At Detective Hart's house this time?"

It wasn't an accusation, so Vi didn't know why it felt like one. "Yes."

"Great. I'll meet you there. We'll plan for nine, but I'll call if it needs to change."

"Sure."

The inspector reached out, gave Vi's shoulder a squeeze. "We're getting to the end, Ms. Reynolds."

Vi swallowed. Hope seemed too dangerous a thing, but it was there. Flapping its wings in her chest. "I hope so."

Chapter Twelve

Thomas headed home from the station. He was running a little late, but he didn't mind showing up at these kinds of Carson and Delaney chaos get-togethers a little late. He was surprised to find Vi pulling up to his house about the same time as him. He hoped that meant her meeting went well.

"You sure look pretty," he said in greeting.

"Is it okay?" she asked, doing a little twirl.

"Of course."

"No, I mean, will it fit in?"

"Sure."

"Ugh. Men." She rolled her eyes. "Mags is asleep. I can just sit with her in the car if you want to go get ready and grab the present."

"Sure, but how'd the meeting with the inspector go?"

She scrunched up her nose. "I don't know that I really had any answers that helped, but she said she's questioning Eric Monday. She seems to think it's all leading to his arrest."

"You don't seem relieved by that?"

"I want to be, but I guess I've seen him get out of too many things to fully believe it until he's behind bars."

"That's fair."

"She wants to meet me at your house at nine on Tuesday to ask me a few more questions, but she seems to think she'll have a warrant by then."

Thomas scowled at that. "I've got court again." And it was incredibly important this time. Allen Scott's initial assault and battery trial, which could lead to reopening his wife's "suicide" case.

"That's okay. I can handle it." And she sounded like she could. Like she wanted to. Every day she seemed more... determined to see everything through. To live in spite of it. Really live, not just hide out at the ranch, or even in his house.

It would have never lasted. She wanted too much for her daughter. So he knew her growth there didn't have anything to do with him. He didn't need it to, as long as she understood that it was really something that she'd managed.

"I'm proud of you, Vi. I hope you know that."

Her mouth curved. "Well, that's sweet, but talking to some postal inspector is hardly much of anything."

"It's everything." He pulled her close, kissed her temple. "I'll be right back." He went to change and grab the present. If Mags woke up, she'd be fussy in the car and want out of her car seat, so he tried to hurry.

In under fifteen minutes, he was driving them out to Cam and Hilly's house. Thomas tried to prepare Vi for the onslaught of people—some she'd know of, some she might even recognize from high school, but mostly it was a whole horde of people who all knew who *she* was, and she didn't really know.

Cam Delaney had built a house just outside of town, and the driveway and road in front of it were filled with cars. Balloons and streamers decorated the outside of the house, and a big arrow sign directed people into the huge backyard, enclosed on all sides by pine trees and then mountains.

Thomas looked in the back seat at Magnolia, who was blinking her eyes open and yawning.

"We're here, sweets. At the party."

"Party," she repeated, smiling and kicking her legs a little.

Thomas got out of the car and moved to get Mags out of her car seat before Vi could. He unbuckled her, then pulled her out and settled her on his hip. She dropped her sleepy head to his shoulder, warm and somewhat sweaty, but it was weird how when it was a little kid, who somehow held your entire heart in her tiny, pudgy hands, that feeling was nice instead of vaguely gross.

He could hear the commotion of the party from here, so he wound his free arm around Vi's waist and led her into the back and the *fray.*

Thomas dropped off the present with Hilly, introduced her and Cam to Vi and Magnolia. He saw Laurel and Grady and their crew with Zach and Lucy and theirs, and started making his way over. They had to stop, make multiple introductions along the way.

Including to Ty and Jen Carson. Which wouldn't have been weird, because he'd literally gone on *maybe* a handful of dates with Jen almost *ten* years ago. But, as they walked away, he *felt* Vi studying him.

"Jen and Laurel look a *lot* alike," Vi said once Jen was out of earshot.

He gave her a sideways glance. "I guess."

She laughed and shook her head. "I bet you were *so* transparent."

"Hey, *she* went on the dates," he replied, leading Vi over to Laurel.

It was kind of funny, because he was just always with the same people all the time, so he forgot things that had once been surprising. Like Daisy Delaney walking among them not using her stage name here. Like the Carson and Delaney feud that used to be the talk of Bent, like how mismatched Laurel and Grady *appeared*, even though he knew they were perfect for each other.

He introduced Vi to Grady, tried not to laugh when she kept surreptitiously looking at Grady's sleeve of tattoos, and then Laurel's sunny ponytail and trim and tidy outfit, as if trying to figure out a complex math equation.

Mags was awake and alert now and demanded to be put down. She watched another group of kids from between Thomas's legs with avid eyes.

Laurel's oldest raced over, her cousin-shadow Fern not far behind.

"What's her name?" Avery demanded of Thomas, pointing at Mags. Then making a funny face at her and making Mags giggle.

"Magnolia."

"She can come play with us," she said to Thomas, then looked at Vi with assessing eyes. "I'm the *best* with babies," Avery said with all the confidence of an oldest girl. "And Fern is second best."

Thomas looked at Vi. She was studying the makeshift playground the kids were playing on. Most of the little ones were being herded by older ones.

Vi offered Avery a smile. "Well, as long as I've got the first and second best to watch after her, I guess it's okay."

Avery held out her hand, and Magnolia took it without much shyness. Then Fern offered her hand and Mags took it with her free one. Then they walked her over to the other kids.

"She's very into the whole babysitting thing right now," Laurel told Vi. "Which she's discovered is basically a way she can boss everyone around."

"Which is not something Avery ever tires of. I don't know where she gets it," Grady drawled, earning him a sharp look from Laurel. But it softened, because little baby Cary was tucked into his arm.

They chatted for a bit, mostly about the kids. Thomas got Vi a plate of food, then maneuvered it so Hilly started talking about nursing school to Vi. He kept an eye on the girls watching Mags and the other kids. The older girls would do a good job, but still he found himself looking over at her just as much if not more than Vi during her conversation with Hilly.

Thomas helped himself to some food, and once he'd gotten his plate full, he saw Laurel approaching him.

"Hide me so I can eat in peace," she said, standing behind him. She grabbed a plate and started to fill it. "Sunny is in a mama-only phase, and it's going to end me."

"That's what you said when Ward was doing the same thing and you survived. And then went on to have two more."

"Some friend you are," she said, taking a big bite of her hot dog.

But Thomas dutifully hid her. He glanced at Mags who was happily watching Fern with big, admiring eyes. Then he glanced at Vi, deep in conversation with Hilly, sunlight dappling her hair burnished copper.

He just couldn't take his eyes off her. Couldn't concentrate on anything else except how much he wanted this. This right here. Every day. Forever.

"Hey, what day do you have free after work this week?" he said to Laurel.

"Why?" she asked, through a mouthful of potato salad.

"I need some help."

"With what?"

"Buying a ring."

She made a noise perilously close to a squeal that had Grady looking over at her, but she waved him off and grabbed Thomas's arm. Shook it.

"Chill out," he muttered.

"Chill out? You're going to ask her to *marry* you."

"Firstly, *shh*. Secondly, maybe. It's too soon. I know it's too soon. I just… But if I had a ring, then… Well, I could be ready. Whenever. Soon. Not soon. I don't know."

"Monday Grady's helping out at the saloon so I've got the kids once I'm off work. But Tuesday I could manage it."

"Okay. Tuesday it is."

Vi CONSIDERED THE whole baby shower thing a success, if only because Thomas had been in a great mood ever since. And okay, it had been a success because Mags had gotten to play with other kids. Vi had gotten to talk to Hilly about nursing and…

And maybe there was a future there. In her old plans. No, she didn't want to be a doctor anymore, but there were a million other healthcare options, and she could hardly spend the rest of her life cowering in other people's houses, hoping cooking and cleaning offered enough to offset her existence.

Maybe thirty-three was a little old to be starting completely over, but she already *had*. What was one more thing?

Monday afternoon, the postal inspector had called her and confirmed their meeting the following morning. She'd been unwilling or unable to give any updates over the phone, and it left Vi with a mix of dread and anxiety.

She tried not to let any of that show, but Thomas seemed to see right through her.

He was dressed in a suit for his day in court, and studied her with concern in his eyes. "Maybe I should be here."

Vi straightened his tie for him. "Don't be ridiculous. You weren't here last time, and I handled it. Besides, if you don't go to court, doesn't that hurt the case?"

He didn't say anything to that, and she knew how important this case was to him. He hadn't given her a lot of specifics, but she knew it was the woman who'd been assaulted the night Eric had last texted her. She knew Thomas thought this was an important step toward proving the man also killed his wife.

"I'll text you right when we're done with all the details. Franny's going to take Mags out for breakfast, then maybe to the park if the weather cooperates. I'll meet them there after the meeting with the inspector. I might head out to the ranch, but I'll let you know if I do."

"Right. Well, that would be good. Going to the ranch, I mean." He smiled, but there was something *odd* about it. "I might be a little late tonight."

She stared at him, something strange and foreign in her gut. At least foreign when it came to Thomas.

She was pretty sure he was lying.

But why would he lie to her about being late? Something with the case? Maybe he just was keeping details of it away from her since it was a domestic assault.

"I have to go. Make sure it's Franny and the postal inspector at the door before you open it, okay?"

Vi nodded. He leaned in, gave her the usual kiss goodbye. Then scooped up Mags until she squealed in delight.

Usual. Because this was usual and their life and she needed to stop being paranoid. Thomas didn't *lie*. Not to her.

He put Magnolia back down, grabbed his bag, and then was off, reminding her to lock the door behind him.

Franny arrived on time as promised. Mags was babbling a mile a minute as they left. Then Vi was left in Thomas's house alone. Everything was quiet.

Too quiet. Too much space for her thoughts to whirl. Worry that Eric wriggled out of whatever he almost had pinned on him. Worry that Thomas was lying about something weird.

So, she threw herself into deep-cleaning the kitchen until her alarm went off, giving her a five-minute warning before the inspector was to arrive. She cleaned herself up a little bit, and the doorbell rang, two minutes before nine.

Vi dutifully checked her phone—where Thomas had added the security app so she could see the door camera as well. Standing on the stoop was the postal inspector, just as she was supposed to be.

Vi opened the door, greeted the inspector and managed a smile as she invited her in. But as Inspector Kay passed, Vi couldn't help but stare.

The inspector had a black eye. Oh, it was covered up with makeup, but Vi knew the telltale signs.

Inspector Kay smiled ruefully, gestured at her eye. "Occupational hazard."

Which means it had happened at work, and she *had* said she was questioning Eric. To Vi, the only logical leap was: "Did Eric do that?"

For a moment, the inspector stood totally still, looking at her with wide eyes. "What?" she said, sounding strange... guilty.

Well, the inspector *had* said that thing about *letting* Eric hit her. Maybe this was her first time suffering from a physical assault. Maybe she had the same shame coursing through her that Vi had once had.

"When you questioned him?" Vi offered, trying to sound soft and kind and understanding. All the things she wished she'd been brave enough to ask for. "Did he hit you?"

"Oh." Dianne lifted a hand to her eye, let out a weird, breathy laugh. "No. He tried to, though. In the scuffle, I got an accidental elbow to the eye from someone trying to restrain him." She shrugged it away. "It happens. But you'll be happy to know, Mr. Carter is under arrest."

"Arrest." The breath simply whooshed out of her and she thought her knees might buckle.

The inspector nodded, heading for the table where they'd had their first meeting. Vi trailed after her, trying to absorb those words.

Arrested. *Arrested.* "In Virginia?"

The inspector put a bag on the table. "I just have a few questions for you, Ms. Reynolds, and then you maybe never have to see me again." She smiled brightly at Vi, but Vi couldn't quite take her gaze off the puffiness around the woman's eye.

"But what did you arrest him for?" Vi asked, walking over to the table, but unable to get herself to sit. "How long will he be in jail? Will there be a trial? I have so many questions."

"Of course you do." The inspector gestured at the chair across from her.

Finally, Vi forced herself to sit. Breathe. Even if she didn't have all the details, it was good. It was… "Are you certain? That he's been arrested? That he's in jail?"

Inspector Kay studied her intently. "Let's focus on the questions *I* need answered first. Does the name Elgie Doyle mean anything to you?"

Vi didn't know how she was supposed to focus when the inspector wouldn't answer a very basic question, but she searched the recesses of her brain for any way that name sounded familiar. She came up empty. "No. Should it?"

The inspector tapped something on her watch, then her gaze turned to Vi. Something about it made Vi…want to run.

Don't be ridiculous and paranoid.

"Not necessarily," Inspector Kay said. "What about the name Burton Slade?"

Now *that* one… It rang some vague bells. "A friend of Eric's, right? But he moved to…" Vi trailed off. Texas. She remembered going to the little farewell party the precinct had thrown him.

For a moment, Vi couldn't catch her breath.

"It's very good of you to want to be so cooperative. It's a shame you recognize the name," the inspector said. Kind tone and smile still in place.

"A shame?"

"Yes, because now we'll have to do this the hard way." Still with that kind smile in place, Inspector Kay pulled a gun out of her bag.

And pointed it right at Vi.

Chapter Thirteen

Thomas hated defense attorneys on a *good* day, and the day Allen Scott tried to weasel out of a clear-cut domestic battery case was *not* a good day. "I hate that guy," Thomas muttered as he walked out of the courthouse for a lunch break.

"He's just doing his job," Laurel offered. The prosecutor wanted her on the stand over a previous case she'd been involved with that tied Scott to the victim.

"You won't be saying that this afternoon when you're up there and he's trying to trip you up on what can be *proven* on body cam footage."

"I sure won't," she agreed with a smile. "You know we could take a lunch and stop by the jewelry store now," Laurel said.

It was a good idea, but Thomas was distracted. His phone screen had no alerts. He didn't have any texts or messages from Vi, and considering how long he'd been in the courtroom, he should.

"Vi didn't text me what happened with the postal inspector."

"Maybe she forgot."

"Maybe, but that's not like her."

"Maybe it's bad news she doesn't want to text you. She wants to tell you in person."

"Yeah, maybe." But it still didn't feel right. He called her. The phone went to voicemail. Then he clicked the location finder. She'd been fine with him tracking her phone, as long as she got to track his. The problem was, if the phone was off or in use, no location came up.

And that was exactly what happened. "I don't like this," he grumbled. He checked the time. "I'm going to swing by my house. I'll just grab a sandwich there."

"Sure," Laurel agreed easily. "We don't have time to split, so I'll just come with if you're worried."

"Yeah. I'm going to call Franny. She was supposed to meet Vi for lu—" Before he even managed to go into his contacts, his phone rang. Sadly, it wasn't Vi.

But it *was* Franny. Maybe Vi's phone wasn't working.

"Franny?" he answered.

"Hey, Thomas. Sorry to bother you. Have you heard from Vi? She was supposed to meet me at the park at noon, and she isn't answering her phone. I could go by your house, but if she's still meeting with the postal inspector, I didn't want to barge in. She's only ten minutes late, so…"

His whole body went ice-cold. If she missed meeting up with Franny and Mags, and wasn't answering her phone, something was *wrong*. Even if it was only ten minutes.

He got in the patrol car, motioned for Laurel to do the same . "I need you to do me a favor, Franny. Just…stay put or head back to the ranch. I'll catch you up once I get to the bottom of things."

"Is something wrong?"

He wanted to lie, but there was no good lie for it. "I'm not sure. Look, I'm on it now. Can you just take Mags to the ranch and focus on taking care of her? I'll focus on finding Vi."

There was a brief pause, but he didn't have time for it.

"Please, Franny. I've got to go." He hung up, prayed like hell Franny would listen, then pulled up the doorbell camera app on his phone.

He watched the footage in double time. "The inspector leaves." He checked the time stamp. "Nine fifteen. Adds up. But then there's nothing. Vi doesn't leave."

"Then she's at home," Laurel said. "We'll drive out. In the meantime, who's close by that's home that could stop in?"

"I'll call Zach and Cam." He started the engine, pulled out of the parking lot. "Their office isn't even a ten-minute drive from my place."

"If they're there and not out on a job. I'll text them. You call...Lucy. Her and Zach are still above the general store, right?"

"Yeah, but she'll have Cooper to wrangle."

"You know what? I'll send out a full Carson-Delaney family text. *Someone* will be free to go pop by and see if everything's okay."

"It could be dangerous."

"She didn't leave the house or it would have shown up on your doorbell camera. And no one besides the inspector went *in* the house, so... It's just... Maybe something happened to her phone."

And maybe something happened to her. But Laurel was right. There was no clear sign of anything...

"You know what? While I text, you call the postal inspector. Maybe see if she'll tell you about the meeting."

"Good idea." He flipped on the lights and sirens, which would make a phone call impossible. "But we're going to get to my house first."

He drove like hell from the courthouse, and toward his house. When his phone sounded—a sign that someone was at his front door on the doorbell camera—Laurel picked up his phone.

"It's just Lucy and Cooper, ringing the bell." Laurel watched the screen and Thomas focused on the road, since he was running code. They were maybe fifteen minutes out still.

"She didn't answer," Laurel said. She kept her voice perfectly calm, but Thomas knew her well enough to know she wasn't as breezy about this whole thing as she had been.

Ten minutes speeding up to and then through Bent felt like *hours* with this worry making his muscles so tight they *ached*.

He pulled up to the house with a screech. Lucy was playing with Cooper in the yard, Mr. Marigold was standing on his side of the fence, clearly chatting with her. "Call the postal inspector," he told Laurel, already out the door and jogging up the walk to his front door.

"Thanks for trying, Lucy," he offered somewhat half-heartedly. He had his keys out and unlocked the door in record time. "You guys should go home," he called.

Maybe it was a mistake, maybe it wasn't dangerous, but it was no place for a kid.

"Vi?" he called out. Too many thoughts assaulted him. Calls he'd answered as a deputy—falls, accidental deaths, natural deaths. Always a family member who'd just... stopped responding.

But she didn't answer, and as he moved through the house, it was clear she wasn't in it. She wasn't *here*.

He forced himself to stop. Breathe. Look around. Was anything out of place?

Not really. It looked exactly like he'd left it. The kitchen was sparkling clean, but she'd no doubt stress-cleaned before the postal inspector had arrived. She'd even put the highchair away so that it looked like a kid didn't live here.

"Damn it, Vi. Where are you?" he muttered. He went through one more search, ending up right back at the front door.

Which was when he realized Vi's purse was still on the hook by the door, and when he opened the purse, her phone was in there.

Laurel came to stand in the front door. "I sent Lucy and Cooper home."

"Good."

"She didn't see anything out of the ordinary. I talked to your neighbor, and he didn't see anything either. Postal inspector's phone was off, but I left a message."

Thomas nodded. "Vi's stuff is still here," he said, pointing at the purse.

Laurel eyed it. "Well, maybe—"

"Her phone is still in it."

Laurel cursed again. "Okay. Let's look through the house. Not just big things, even the tiniest things. Kitchen's as clean as I've ever seen it."

"She cleans when she's stressed," Thomas muttered. He didn't want to go through the house again. He wanted to go around in a rage, screaming for her from the rooftops. But Laurel was right. The smart thing to do was to go over the house one more time.

"She must have cleaned before the inspector got here. Everything out here looks pristine." He took the hallway, pointed into the bathroom. He studied the sink, the shower, the towel hanging on the rack—where he'd put it this morning. "Her stuff is where it usually is. So is mine, and Magnolia's." He moved down to the bedroom. Flipped on the light. "Bed's made—that's all her. Closet is closed, just like she usually closes it." He paused, then heard something odd. And saw the curtain flutter.

"Wait." He strode over to the curtains, jerked them back. The window was open. "I didn't leave this window open." He peered out, realized it wasn't just an open window, the screen had been popped out. And carefully leaned against the side of the house.

He and Laurel swore in unison.

Thomas was about to jump out the window himself, but Laurel grabbed him. "We'll call in Copeland. Have him bring out the fingerprint kit. So go around the front. We don't want to contaminate the scene."

She had her phone out and was dialing already. "Breathe, Thomas. Breathe," she said, and then Copeland must have answered, because Laurel started barking orders. She reached out to him, squeezed his arm.

"Any idea what she's wearing?"

"No. She would have changed for the meeting with the inspector."

Laurel put her mouth back toward the receiver. "No purse. No phone. We're going to canvass the neighborhood. You get what you need to print the house, then get out here. Call the postal inspector on your way. As far as we know, she would have been the last one to see Vi."

Copeland must have agreed, because Laurel ended the phone call, then turned to Thomas. She was calm. She was in control, and it helped him remember he needed to find that calm and cool too.

Maybe it was Vi. Maybe he was terrified, but it was a case like any other.

He had to think of it that way.

VI LAY IN the back seat of the postal inspector's rental car in stillness and tried to see what she could out of the window as the inspector drove. Mostly, she just saw sky, but if she could catch a glimpse of the tops of mountains, she at least would know what direction they were driving in.

She was pretty sure they'd headed south-ish out of town. She could be wrong, because really there wasn't much south of Bent. Ranches and small towns. Sunrise, eventually.

Her wrists and ankles were zip-tied, so she knew there was no getting out of the bonds, but if she could have some idea of where she was, then she still had a chance.

Except, small towns and ranches meant plenty of places to hide.

Plenty of places to dump a body.

She blew out a breath. *We're not going to think like that*, she told herself sternly. A trick she'd learned in therapy when her thoughts spiraled to blaming herself for Eric's abuse. Usually she said it out loud, but with the postal inspector right there in the driver's seat, Vi kept all words internal.

Maybe she should have fought her. Maybe she should have taken the chance. But the inspector had given her a choice—leave with her out the bedroom window, or they could sit there and wait for Thomas to come home and she would shoot him in the head when he walked in the door.

Maybe it had been a bluff. Maybe Vi should have called it.

But she thought about his story with the dime, how he'd already narrowly escaped a gunshot wound to the head once. She just hadn't been able to take that kind of chance.

So, she'd let the zip ties be put on her wrists. The only thing Vi had bothered to ask was if the woman was really a postal inspector. Dianne had just laughed and tightened the zip ties.

Vi didn't know what that meant, really. She supposed it didn't matter.

She'd let the lady pull her through the house, into the bedroom, then the woman had opened the window and pushed her out.

Vi's ankle had rolled on impact and it ached even now, but she was well-versed in aches you had to just live through.

She was going to find a way to live through this. She had a daughter. She had a man who loved her. She had *family*, and even if she'd made a mistake in being allowed to be taken to a second location, she would fight.

Because wherever the inspector was taking her was hopefully away from Thomas and anyone else who might get caught in the crossfire.

Maybe she didn't know what the inspector wanted, or why Vi was the target, but she'd fight her like hell...as long as no one else could possibly get hurt.

She tried to keep track of time or miles or *anything* about the car ride, but in the end, she had no idea how long they drove. How far. Even when the inspector pulled the car to a stop, opened the back seat door, and then pulled Vi up and out of the car, Vi didn't know where they were.

Deep in a wooded cove. Mountains seemingly all around them, blocking out the sky. There was a dilapidated-looking cabin a few yards away.

"I don't know why you bothered to bring me all the way out here just to kill me. Thomas is going to find you." Vi was going to believe that was true. She'd been purposefully rude to his neighbor who had stopped her and Dianne, because she knew Mrs...well, whatever her name was, was a bit of a busybody and always bothering Thomas with silly neighborhood disputes.

If the neighbor didn't go running to tell him about the car and the woman with her, Vi would eat her hat. She'd only wished the inspector had put the zip ties on her ankles at that point, but the inspector had made sure it looked like she was walking around of her own volition.

The inspector didn't really say anything as she pulled Vi out of the car. She just pointed at the cabin, gave Vi a careful nudge—because too hard of one would send her toppling. "Let's go."

The inspector had her elbow and was trying to move her forward at the snail's pace required of having her ankles tied together.

Vi eyed the cabin. It looked like it had been abandoned *decades* ago.

"I'm not going in there."

"Yes, you are," the inspector said, pulling her by the elbow.

But Vi had a one-year-old. She knew all about dead weight. So she simply dropped to the ground. When the inspector just grabbed her by the wrists and began to painfully drag her across the ground, Vi bucked and wriggled and did everything she could to get the inspector off her.

The woman just grunted and fought right back, and since she had free hands and apparently impressive strength, she kept making progress toward the cabin.

Vi tried not to feel defeated, but by the time they reached the one stair up to the porch, and the inspector used two hands to painfully jerk her over it and onto the porch, Vi didn't know what she was going to accomplish trying to fight anyone, all tied up the way she was.

"On your feet." The inspector jerked her up. Vi considered just flopping back on the ground, but what did that do? Maybe if she was upright there'd be some way to kind of throw herself into the inspector. Push her in some way.

The inspector shoved the cabin door open and pulled

Vi inside behind her. Immediately, Vi heard someone else. Someone already in the cabin. When her eyes adjusted to the darkness, she saw a figure sitting at the table.

"Hello, Vi."

Vi didn't say anything in response. She immediately turned and tried to escape.

Chapter Fourteen

Thomas figured the cold, empty feeling inside of him was good. It meant he wasn't freaking out. If he was tethered to his body, he might start tearing his house apart piece by damn piece. Until he found a clue.

Right now, he stood in the side yard next to Laurel, studying his open window. Copeland hadn't shown up yet, but Thomas had to believe it would be soon.

Had to.

"Look," Laurel said. "We talked to your other neighbors, watched your doorbell cam footage from front and back doors, but we didn't talk to anyone in the back. If no one facing the street saw them, if none of the cameras caught them, they had to go somewhere outside those things." Laurel pointed behind him, where his backyard backed up to neighbor's backyards.

"If she came out the side window, she could go that way, and the camera wouldn't pick it up."

Thomas was halfway across the yard before Laurel was even done talking. He talked to all his neighbors as a matter of course. A lot of the older ones had sought *him* out, with their variety of "complaints" about the neighborhood and what he could do to solve them in a law enforcement capacity.

His backyard catty-corner neighbor was one of the people who loved to complain the most. If Vi had gone through her yard in any capacity, Mrs. Harolds would know.

He was at her front door in seconds flat and had to remind himself not to bang on the door like a man determined to break it down. Just three sharp knocks.

He counted in his head, trying to keep from kicking the door open. When it finally did, Mrs. Harolds stood on the other side of her storm door.

"Oh, hello, Thomas. Well, aren't you dressed up nice? You know, I'm glad you stopped by."

"Mrs. Harolds—"

But she kept talking, opening the storm door and stepping out onto the porch as Laurel came up behind him.

"That girlfriend of yours was *very* rude to me."

Thomas thought his knees might give out. "Today? You saw Vi this morning?"

"Yes." She pointed out toward her perfectly manicured lawn and beautiful gardens. "There was a car parked in front of my mailbox when I went out to check on my roses. Then her and her friend started to get in. Well, I told them not to park in front of my mailbox, because the mailman always gets a bit prickly about it and won't deliver my mail, and I'm expecting a very important package."

Thomas nodded, trying to absorb this information. A car parked in front of Mrs. Harolds's house. There was no reason for that, except sneaking around.

"She didn't even apologize. She told me to mind my own business. Can you believe it?"

"What kind of car? Can you describe the friend?"

Mrs. Harolds frowned. "It was *very* rude."

"Yes, Mrs. Harolds," Laurel said, before Thomas could explode on the older woman. "What kind of car?"

"I took a picture of it. I know you told me that the police

can't help me just because someone parks in front of my mailbox, but *I* was going to report it anyway. Hold on."

She disappeared inside and Thomas had to clench his hands into fists to keep from barging in after her.

Laurel put her hand on his shoulder. "It's a lead. It's a start. Any idea who the friend might be?"

"None. She was supposed to be meeting Franny and Mags at the park."

Mrs. Harolds reappeared with her phone and held it out to him. "Her friend was driving. So, I suppose it was her friend's car, but still. She could have said sorry. *She* knows me. The other woman doesn't. And isn't from around here, far as I can tell."

Laurel peered over his shoulder at the photo of a navy blue sedan. He couldn't make out anything going on inside the car.

"Rental car," Laurel said, pointing to the sticker on the back that indicated it was from the rental company. "I'll text the plate to Copeland. Someone can get in touch with the rental company."

Thomas nodded. "Can you describe her friend?" he asked Mrs. Harolds.

"She was dressed much nicer than Vi. You know, I don't know why young women wear those jeans. In my generation, we got dressed up if we were going anywhere. We cared about our appearance."

Thomas wanted to scream, but he kept his cool. It was the only way to get the information. "And the friend did? Was she wearing a dress?"

"No, she looked very professional. Like Laurel here," Mrs. Harolds said, pointing to Laurel's court outfit. A blazer, button-up, and modest skirt. "Dark hair, pulled back.

Dark sunglasses. I thought maybe she was a cop, though I didn't recognize her."

"Okay." There were no other female cops in the department who'd be out of uniform. Could it have been one of the municipalities in Bent County? Except why would they come this way, and why wouldn't Vi *call* him?

"Thank you. You've got my number right, Mrs. Harolds? If you think of anything else, if you see that car again, can you call me? Right away."

"Well, of course. I'd like to see them punished for blocking a mailbox."

He narrowly resisted telling her he didn't give a shit about her mailbox. Probably because Laurel was pulling him away. Back through Mrs. Harolds's backyard and then his own. Copeland was just pulling up with a deputy in a county van.

"I'll show Bridgers where to get the prints from," Laurel said. She motioned for the deputy to follow her inside once he had his toolbox.

"I've got Clarion working on dealing with the rental company," Copeland said to him. "Once we know who rented it out, it'll go over the radio."

"She's with a woman. Dark hair. Blazer, skirt. No idea height or weight. No idea anything beyond that car."

"Then we'll get to the bottom of that car. Hey." Copeland studied him. "Listen, I know you want to be a part of this—"

"You aren't about to suggest I sit this out?"

"Sit out the case involving your live-in girlfriend? Me? No. Why would I do that?"

Thomas scowled at him. "I'm letting you and Laurel take the lead as best I can. But I have to be here. I have to be part of this."

"Look. I'm going to ask this, because it has to be asked. Because Laurel's got too soft a spot for you to do it, but someone's got to. Is it possible she left of her own accord?"

Thomas wanted to be offended. He *was* offended. But he was also still numb enough to know Copeland was just doing his job.

"Even if I take myself out of this, she wouldn't leave her daughter, her cousins without a word. She just wouldn't." Speaking of cousins… "I'm going to call Rosalie while you guys process the house."

"You sure you want to bring a bunch of reckless PIs into this?"

He already had pushed in Rosalie's number and was listening to the phone ring in his ear. "Yeah, I'm sure."

Vi HADN'T GOTTEN more than one step before she fell. All on her own. Like an idiot. But panic had shot through her with such a violent surge of shock, she hadn't thought. She'd only acted.

Eric was here. Working with the inspector? How? *Why?*

"Dianne," he said, in that terrible, patient way of his. The kind she knew meant terrible things were coming. "Get her on her feet."

The inspector yanked Vi up again. "Where do you think you're going tied up like that?" She laughed, the sound full of menace, not humor.

Vi looked up at the woman, wondering how this had happened. "You said he was arrested."

"I lied." *Dianne* shrugged. "Like you should have." She shoved Vi forward, and then into a chair. Facing Eric. Who just sat there, looking calm and still as he so often did. If there was anything *off* about him, it was the faint hint of a beard growing and the fact his hair was a little long. In all their time together, he'd preferred to stay clean-shaven with a short buzz cut.

He looked at her, nothing but smug satisfaction in his expression. Just like when she'd tried to go to the police the first time, and nothing had come of it.

It lit something within her. An anger that she'd had to push down deep when she'd been with him for fear that everything would spiral out of control. An anger she'd avoided out of fear for so long.

But these past two years, she'd climbed out of fear. So anger and temper snapped inside of her like a storm.

"Well, Eric, this might be the stupidest thing you've ever done."

Some of that smug melted off his face. "What did you say?"

"You heard me."

"And I want you to repeat it. Word for word." He stood, using his height and his overmuscled, compact body to create a threat. Looming over her, the table between them.

Two responses warred within her. The old one where she said nothing, kept her eyes downcast, and prayed he stopped. *Prayed* he would just stop caring anything about her and leave her to her survival.

Then a new one, where she held his gaze, said all the reckless things cluttering up her mind, and took whatever he dished out.

"This is the stupidest—"

He lifted the table and hurled it so that it crashed into the wall, one of the legs knocking against her knee on its way.

She swallowed down the yelp of pain and she did *not* look down. "—thing you've ever done."

"You know I hate that word, Vi." Because *his* father had called him stupid. *His* father had beaten him, and she'd let that sympathy keep her for far too long in a terrible, dangerous situation. She thought she could break the cycle of abuse.

He made *sure* she thought she could, she realized in retrospect. He'd known how to use the sob story of his childhood to keep her tricked and trapped.

"I do know," Vi said. "That's why I used it." Then she squeezed her eyes shut and braced herself for the backhand. The stomach punch. Whatever horrible blow was coming.

When nothing happened, she opened her eyes. Eric was still hovering above her. *Smirking.* His hand was in a fist, reared back and ready to do damage. But for the time being, he was just watching her.

He got off on the fear. On the cowering. And she'd given him that, year after year. Always convincing herself it was self-protection.

Maybe it had been. Maybe if she'd stood up to him then, she'd be dead, and Magnolia would have never been born, and Thomas...

It was an alternate reality worse than this one. This one where he'd somehow gotten the postal inspector to *kidnap* her. She looked at Dianne. "Why are you doing this?"

Eric looked over at the woman. "You know, Dianne here is a perfect example of what a woman *should* be to the man who loves her. Loyal. Willing to go above and beyond to make her man happy." Eric reached out, ran a hand over Dianne's hair.

Like they were intimate. Like he cared. She might have even believed it if she believed he was capable.

"Once you're out of the way, we're going to get married," Dianne said, wrapping her arm around Eric's waist. She looked down at Vi like that was some kind of great injury. "If you hadn't come up with that connection to Texas, we might have let you go. But…" Dianne shrugged as if this was all Vi's fault.

The fact she'd let him make her feel at fault for so long burned like acid in her gut. "You have a new wife lined up, then. Congratulations. Enjoy hell, Dianne." She glared at Eric. "So why aren't you killing me and getting it over with?"

Eric leaned in close, some horrible mix of sneer and grin on his face. He smelled like beer and sweat and it made her want to retch.

"Do you know how long I can draw this out?" he said. "How much I can make you hurt and suffer for *weeks*? And no one. *No one* will find you. *No one* will stop me. I never would have killed you, Vi. I would have loved you and taken care of you forever, but then you left. You brought this upon yourself."

The fact he could even *pretend* he had loved her baffled her. "Do you really believe that?"

"If you'd learned how to be a better wife, I wouldn't have had to hurt you the way I did. If you'd kept it to your-self, not tried to drag my entire precinct into it, every-thing would have been *fine*. If you'd stayed, we could have worked things out. But you ran. So now you have to pay."

But he'd had all this time. All this space. And still, she was sitting here breathing.

"I'm going to torture you, Vi," he said, seeming to get im-mense physical pleasure just from saying those words. "As long as I can draw it out. We're in the middle of nowhere— thanks for the idea, by the way. I couldn't have found any-where as isolated as Bent County if I tried."

She knew he meant it as a threat, but it sent a bolt of hope through her. She was still in Bent County. That meant she still had a chance. A hope.

Because Thomas would find a way. She knew he'd find a way. Maybe he'd be too late, and that would be horrible... He'd blame himself. He'd...

No, she had to do everything in her power to stay alive. To survive whatever Eric did. If she gave Thomas enough time... She would not be the corpse he found. She *wouldn't*.

"No one's saving you from me, Vi." Eric grabbed her by the neck, squeezed until she was struggling to suck in a breath. *"No one."*

Thomas will, she told herself. And she held on to that belief as hard as she could.

Chapter Fifteen

Thomas hung up with Rosalie. She was going to try some not strictly legal methods of determining Eric Carter's whereabouts and report back to him. He was glad to have more eyes on this, but mostly felt a sick tangle of guilt over worrying Rosalie. Over all the ways he'd failed this.

Failed.

Where the hell was she? Who was this friend? The only thing that kept him from going absolutely ballistic was that Mrs. Harolds had said the friend, the driver of the car, was a woman.

Not that women couldn't hurt people, but it wasn't Vi's ex-husband. If Rosalie came back with absolute proof Eric Carter was in Virginia and had no connection to this, maybe… Maybe it was all a misunderstanding.

He wanted to believe that more than he wanted to take his next breath.

He tried to stay out of the way of everyone processing the house. He let Laurel and Copeland make the phone calls. He focused on his notebook, writing down a list of everything he could think of that would need to be done. Then he'd go through each piece, one by one, until she was found.

She was going to be found.

Thomas wasn't sure how many hours passed of seeming

nothingness, but eventually Copeland and Laurel came to where he'd situated himself at his kitchen table. Notepad and phone in front of him.

He kept checking it to make sure he hadn't missed a message from her.

"A few updates," Laurel said. And it was her cop-to-victim voice, so he knew it was only bad news.

"We got the identity of the person who rented the car," Copeland said. "Dianne Kay. Postal Inspector Dianne Kay."

The postal inspector was the friend? He supposed the description Mrs. Harolds gave matched, but it didn't make any sense. Why had she come back after questioning Vi? Why wouldn't she have gone to the front door? Why would she park on the opposite street? Why would Vi leave out a window to get to her?

He wanted to feel relief, but dread was the winning emotion.

"At least, she *was* a postal inspector," Laurel said. "I called her office, but I was forwarded to a different inspector who told me Dianne Kay put in her two weeks last week. Then didn't show up to work yesterday."

"But…she was working by questioning Vi this morning."

"Apparently not officially," Laurel said. "I talked to her supervisor, trying to get some information on the case she was working on and what it might have to do with leaving with Vi. He wasn't very forthcoming. We'll need warrants and to wade through all kinds of federal red tape."

"We don't have that kind of time."

"We've got an APB out on the car. They put out an emergency ping on the postal inspector's phone, but it's been turned off. I put Vicky on starting to get whatever paperwork we need to get a hold of her case information, and we'll be getting a search warrant to get the inspector's phone location history. Hopefully we find Vi before that matters, but it's good to have it rolling."

"All the deputies have a description of both Vi and Kay, and anyone not on a call is going to be on the lookout for either woman or the car. Day and night shift. It's early to call it a missing person, early to assume this is nefarious, but…"

"But we all damn well know it's nefarious." Thomas pushed out of his seat. He went to stand by the front window. The sun was setting. Most of the police officers had dissipated. Some would be running tests on what they'd found. Some would be going home.

And somewhere out there, Vi was… God, he needed her to be okay.

So he turned back to the table, his list. And as he went over it, he realized there was something they were leaving out. "What about Eric Carter?"

Laurel and Copeland exchanged a look.

"What about him?" Copeland asked.

"Where is he?" Thomas demanded.

"We're still figuring it out," Laurel said calmly. She held up her hand when he all but exploded. "We called his precinct and it's his scheduled day off. We asked them to verify his residence, but the person we talked to refused. So, we're working on getting another agency out to his residence. One we can trust. I've got Zach pulling some FBI strings."

Thomas let out a long, slow breath. FBI strings were good. And it was better this way, because Laurel was right. After everything they'd heard from Vi, they couldn't trust the precinct Eric worked for.

"If he's not there, I want his credit card records pulled immediately. And his cell phone pinged."

"We've got everything set up to do that immediately once we get word."

It was something and it was *nothing*, because it didn't find Vi. And the wheels of justice moved far too slow when people were in danger. He walked away from the table again, needing to move. Just...move. He narrowly missed stepping on a mangled little stuffed animal.

His heart just cracked in two. He picked it up off the floor. "Mags can't sleep without it," he muttered. Franny had taken Magnolia back to the ranch, and they had plenty of stuff out there to get Mags through the night. But...

Laurel held out a hand to take the stuffed animal. "I can drive it out to—"

But Thomas didn't relinquish the lamb. "No, I'll do it."

"You're going to exhaust yourself, Thomas."

He knew Laurel was worried about him. "I have to do it. I have to see... I just have to."

Laurel swallowed. He could see the emotions in her eyes, and he *hated* it. They'd worked too many cases together where the people in trouble were people they loved.

They'd never failed before. He wouldn't fail now. "I'll head out now. Keep me updated."

"Thomas..." But Laurel didn't say anything, and Thomas didn't wait around to hear what she had to say.

There was nothing *to* say. He'd overlooked something. He hadn't been observant or diligent enough, and who suffered? Not him. Vi. *Again.*

He could try to believe she'd left of her own accord. He could try to fool himself into thinking he'd deliver the lamb stuffed animal, and Vi would just be at the ranch. He wished with all his might that she was just tired of him, his overprotectiveness, and...anything. *Anything* that could make this about leaving him and not about being hurt or in danger.

He could suffer through anything else as long as she was okay. He told that to himself, to God, to whatever deities wanted to listen, as he took the long, lonely drive out to the Young Ranch.

But when he pulled up, he hadn't convinced himself of anything. He knew something was deeply wrong, Vi was in danger, and he didn't know how to *fix* it.

So what good was he?

With lead limbs, he got out of the car and trudged up to the front door, lamb in hand. The door flew open before he was even up the porch stairs.

"Is there any news?" Franny demanded.

"I'm sorry, no," Thomas managed, though his voice sounded mangled even to his own ears. "I just wanted Mags to have this tonight." He held out the lamb.

"Tata!" She squealed happily from where she'd been playing with blocks on a rug in the living room. She pulled up on the couch onto her feet and then toddled over to him. He stepped inside so she didn't try to come out. She reached up for him, for her lamb, and he handed her the stuffed animal, picked her up in one fell swoop.

It was worse than being shot.

Worse than anything he'd ever experienced. Her excitement at seeing him, the way she leaned into him, held on, happily babbled to him. When he'd failed her mother, failed *her*.

Still, he closed his eyes, held on and squeezed tight. "I'm sorry, sweets," he whispered. "But I won't stop until she's home."

Vi's throat burned from where Eric had choked her. It made every breath in and out painful.

He was good at that. Always had been. And he'd used it—those hurts and pains no one else could see, that were minor enough to suffer through, as a reminder.

No one crossed Eric Carter.

But she *had* crossed him. Maybe she hadn't been able to put him behind bars, but her *trying* had been enough that it had forced him to agree to the divorce or risk getting out who he was.

She had lived almost two years without him. She'd had a child, and since he hadn't brought Magnolia up, she was almost certain Eric didn't know about her.

That, and Thomas, and her cousins and her friends—new and old, all worked inside her to remind her that she would not fall back into the trap of thinking Eric controlled the world.

She wouldn't go down cowering. She wouldn't go down at all. She would swing and swing and swing, until Thomas found her.

And she shoved aside a niggling fear he wouldn't get here soon enough. She sat in her chair, breathed as easily as she could with the burn in her throat.

On the terrible off chance she didn't escape this, at least everyone would know she'd gone down fighting. This time, she wasn't running away.

She looked from Eric to Dianne and decided that, if nothing else, she was damn well going to get some answers.

"I still don't understand how you two connect."

"We met at a law enforcement conference in Fort Worth," Dianne said with a little smirk. "Four years ago."

Four years. Vi could only stare at Dianne for a moment, and really the smirk made it clear what she meant by four years.

She wanted to laugh, and then thought…what the hell? She let it fly, earning arrested glares from Eric *and* Dianne.

"So, you were cheating on me?" She laughed again. All his talk about love and devotion and… Wow. Just *wow*.

"Maybe if you weren't such a frail little sad sack I wouldn't have had to," Eric shot back.

"Burton introduced us. Eric and I bonded over law enforcement, because I wasn't too stupid to finish school," Dianne said.

But the barb didn't land for a number of reasons, mainly because suddenly Eric's attention was on Dianne. And it was *not* good.

"Shut the hell up," Eric said, giving her a hard shove. She stumbled back a little but caught herself on the wall. Eric followed, hulking above her while she pressed herself against the wall. "What the hell is wrong with you? Are you *stupid*? You don't give the hostage *information*, you useless waste of space."

"I'm sorry," Dianne whispered. Not so smug and happy with herself now.

But he stood there for ticking minutes, menace and violence shimmering in the air around them. Dianne looked at the ground, looked like she was trying to melt into the wall.

Finally, Eric relented. He turned away from her, grabbed a gun that had been propped up in the corner.

"I'm going to go see what I can hunt up for dinner." He dramatically waved around his giant gun. He aimed at Dianne for a moment, cocked his head.

Vi held her breath, and if she wasn't mistaken, Dianne did too.

"You better shut your mouth, Dianne. I don't want to have to hurt you again, but you've made a lot of big mistakes the past few days."

"I'm sorry, Eric."

He grunted, lowered the gun slowly. Then shrugged. "I should be able to get some deer or elk. You better be ready to butcher and cook when I get back."

"I am. I will. I've been practicing."

"You see, Vi," Eric said, turning to her. "A man provides for the woman he loves, and she makes his dinner. He provides. She supports. Why could you never learn that?"

Vi thought of all the dinners she'd made. Reheated. The lunches she'd packed. The breakfasts she'd gotten up early to make from scratch, so he didn't get mad. So he didn't hurt her.

Only now that she was out of it, with the help of Mags and therapy and Thomas and her cousins did she fully understand...

It would have never been enough. She could have been perfect in every way, and he would have found fault. Because *she* was not the problem.

He was.

Once Eric was gone, Vi studied Dianne. Could she get through to her now that Eric was openly threatening her?

Based on Dianne's frantic scrubbing of the kitchen counters, Vi didn't think so. But maybe Vi could show her the truth.

"He gave you that black eye."

Dianne ignored her, but her only chance of actual escape, at least before the police managed to track her down, was to get through to Dianne. "Do you think you can do everything right and he'll stop? Because he won't. This will be you." Vi pointed to herself with both hands, since her wrists were zip-tied together.

Dianne looked down at her haughtily. "I don't believe that. *I* know how to learn a lesson. See? I made a mistake and he didn't hit me, did he? He gave me a warning. Because he knows I can get better."

"He shoved you and held a gun pointed *at* you."

Dianne didn't say anything. Just went back to furious scrubbing.

"There's no lesson to learn. No perfection to claim. He will beat the will to live out of you, and then you'll be wishing he'd just kill you and get it over with."

Dianne whipped a furious gaze at Vi. "You're the one who's going to wind up dead."

"Maybe, but you'll only be next."

"He won't kill me. He *loves* me. And it took a lot for him to trust me after what *you'd* done to him."

"You mean, when I was busy scrubbing his counters terrified he'd come home and beat me again, and you two were apparently having an affair?"

"You don't know what you're talking about."

But Vi absolutely knew exactly what she was talking about. Now she just had to think of what she could say that might get through to Dianne. Was there anything? Was there anything anyone could have said to her to get it through her head that she didn't deserve what Eric was doing to her?

"He'll never come back, you know. That man you first met. Who charmed you. Who *you* thought was building you up, making you forget whatever failure you were mired in." She could see it clearly now, but in the moment she'd only seen someone giving her attention.

Not someone who made sure she knew how little she deserved it. Not someone who knew just what wounds to press on. She'd spent a good amount of years thinking maybe she deserved the abuse if she could be so blind, but to see him do the same thing to someone else, to make a victim out of someone else to the point this woman was willing to hurt other people…

No, she wasn't stupid. No, it wasn't her fault. And if she got out of this, she certainly wasn't going to be worried about anyone thinking that anymore.

Chapter Sixteen

By the time Thomas had left Mags with Franny and Audra and headed back to Bent it was late. He didn't go to his house, for a lot of reasons, but the main one was being there without Vi and Magnolia might just break him. He was barely hanging on as it was.

He went to the station instead. Copeland and Laurel weren't there, but they had been texting him updates, and he knew they were hard at work. Unfortunately, most of the updates were boring, pointless and unhelpful.

They were running the prints. Talking to the hotel where the postal inspector had stayed. Waiting to hear the results of pinging the postal inspector's phone.

So Thomas spent the entire evening leaving messages, sending emails, spreading as wide a net as possible. He asked anyone he knew of with even the tiniest connections to law enforcement to see what they could do. Zach's FBI connections. Jack Hudson, the sheriff of Sunrise, who Thomas had worked with at Bent County when they'd both started out as cops and then again over the past year, when Jack's family had been in some trouble. He was friends with Zeke Daniels, who was pretty tight-lipped about his past, but Thomas knew he had something to do with some secret gang-busting group, so he messaged him too. He even reached out to his cousin's husbands who were former military, to see if they had any ideas.

He thought about driving around with some half-cocked idea that he would just *sense* where Vi was, but it was dark and he was exhausted, and while sleep would be impossible, driving around wasn't smart.

He wasn't going to magically find her like that. It required work, and investigation, and being *smart*. Everyone was working overnight on this. Everyone he trusted. The best detectives he knew.

But he had never been on *this* side of things, not like this. And suddenly he had a lot of empathy for the people in his past who hadn't followed his, at times, black-and-white view of the law and helping people.

Was this his punishment?

He shook that thought away because this wasn't about *him*. It was about Vi. Who had driven off with the postal inspector for some unknown reason. He held on to the tiniest sliver of hope that it might have been of her own volition, for a good reason that would become clear as soon as possible.

Thomas went back to his computer, focusing on Dianne Kay. But there was nothing to indicate a woman who was anything other than what she'd presented herself as. A postal inspector from Texas. And wasn't that good? That Vi was with someone who appeared to be on the up-and-up?

Except for the whole quitting her job thing and questioning Vi when she technically wasn't *on the job.*

He clicked off the monitor with more force than necessary. He needed more coffee, and probably some food. Though he didn't think he could stomach either, but he'd try.

Before he could leave his office, and still far too early for anyone to be awake, Rosalie stormed into his office. "I got some intel for you." She slapped a grainy black-and-white still from a surveillance video to his chest. "That son of a bitch isn't in Virginia."

Thomas took the picture away, stared at it, resisting the urge to crumple it. He could surmise who the *SOB* was just by the violence in Rosalie's tone. "Where was this?"

"Convenience store in Fairmont. *Friday.*"

Thomas swore. Fairmont. *Friday.* Eric Carter was in Wyoming. In Bent County. In the same town the postal inspector had stayed.

He couldn't hear much else beside the hammering beat of his heart echoing in his ears.

Vi's ex-husband was *here*. Close enough to *do* something. Maybe... Maybe the postal inspector had known that. Maybe she was helping Vi.

But Thomas couldn't find a way for that to make sense and ease this slam of terror and fury that the man who'd abused her for years was in his own county.

"Did you find out where he was staying?" Thomas demanded, skirting his desk.

"No. I tracked him to this convenience store using his alias, but as far as I've been able to tell, he hasn't used his credit cards or his alias since that gas and food purchase on Friday. I've got Quinn on it, though, and she'll call me if she finds anything else or anything new comes across."

Thomas had no doubt the way she was going about getting access to credit cards was illegal, but he didn't ask for details.

He grabbed his keys. "Let's go then."

But Rosalie stopped him, arms crossed over her chest, blue eyes wary and assessing.

"Probably best if you stay out of this one, Hart. You've got all those pesky laws to follow."

"I'd break any damn law to find her, Rosalie." Any of

them. "If we take my patrol car, we can ride code all the way to Fairmont."

Rosalie paused for only a second. "All right. Let's go."

ERIC CAME BACK in a foul mood. He hadn't managed to shoot anything, which was hardly a surprise since he didn't know what the hell he was doing. Maybe he was a good shot in the realm of police work, but he'd never hunted anything a day in his life.

Oh to have the unearned confidence of a man.

Vi sat on the chair, wondering if there was anything sharp in this cabin that she could use to cut through the zip ties. She moved her hands this way and that, testing if she had the dexterity to do it. Maybe not the ones on her wrists, but she could do the ones on her ankles.

And then she could run.

Maybe it all *felt* hopeless, but she was determined to trick her brain into only seeing possibilities. *Positive thinking* in the most negative of situations. That was kind of what her therapist had taught her—though for mental spirals, not actual danger.

"Well? Why aren't you making anything for me to eat?" Eric demanded of Dianne. Who jumped up and scurried into the kitchen area.

"I can make you a sandwich."

"A *sandwich*? After the day I've had?" He advanced on her, and she pressed herself against the old, grimy countertop that he had her blocked into.

"I'm sorry," she said desperately. "I just don't know much about cooking. I can bake. I can—"

"If you take these zip ties off me, I can make dinner," Vi interrupted. Because she just…couldn't stand it. It felt like watching a movie of her old life. The fear, the desperation, but so deep in it there was no seeing the abuse and intimidation caused by a warped man—not by her own failures.

Eric turned slowly. He'd always known how to use slow in the most menacing ways. His dark, empty gaze bored into her. But he wasn't turning Dianne into an old scene out of her life anymore, so she relaxed.

For a minute.

Then he started moving toward her. With every step he took, Vi's body reacted. Freezing. Heart tripling its beat. Hands getting clammy. Fear gripping her throat and making it hard to breathe. So that she was no longer *watching* old scenes from her life. She was *feeling* them.

He moved over to her, each step a loud, violent *threat*, and she knew *something* was coming. Even if he didn't hit her right away. He liked to draw it out, to see how afraid he could make her before he snapped.

But she'd just watched him do that to Dianne. She'd just spent two years crawling out of that. So she held his gaze, and tried to hide the physical fear reactions of her body under a cold, unperturbed mask.

He leaned his face in close to hers. He smelled like cheap soap and beer. His face was twisted in fury, an expression she still saw in her nightmares. She was shaking now, no matter how hard she tried to hold herself still.

"Do you think I'm stupid?" he asked in that deceptively mild tone he'd once employed so well. The last line of control before he lost all control. She'd been on this precipice so many times—and there'd been *years* she'd thought she controlled the outcome. That if she did the right thing, he wouldn't fall over the edge and take her with him.

She'd been so very wrong.

Physically, she recoiled. Everything inside her trembled

because her body knew. What would come. That there was nothing she could do about it.

But her mind also knew a thing or two she'd learned over the course of these past two years. She fought the old self-preservation instinct to look down, cower away.

She would never cower to this man again.

"Stupid?" she asked lightly, and even though her hands shook, her voice was clear and strong. "I'm banking on it."

The blow was swift, vicious. Hard in her stomach, under her rib cage. Right where it would do a considerable amount of damage. The pain shouldn't be shocking. She'd spent so many years suffering under this man's blows.

And still, she hadn't braced herself in quite the right way. The force of the blow had the chair she was sitting in toppling backward and splintering into pieces. She fell to the ground and pain shot through her shoulder blade as chair hit floor, and shoulder hit the edge of the chair back. Then the back of her skull erupted in pain as the force of impact made her head snap back onto the floor.

Then he was standing over her, a foot on either side of her hip. He kicked a part of the chair out of the way, and she couldn't stop herself from flinching. He sneered down at her. He was wavering a little bit—the blow to her head hard enough to make her vision feel off.

"I wish I could let them find your body, Vi. Because every inch of it will be bruised and bloodied once I'm done. It's a shame you're just going to disappear forever."

She didn't say anything else. She might have if so much pain wasn't throbbing through her body. The knock to her head made her dizzy and nauseous. She couldn't really concentrate on him standing over her.

She should have. She should have remembered.

He grabbed her by the hair, laughed when she howled

in pain as he jerked her by the hair out of the chair and off the floor and onto her knees.

"That's better," he said.

He released her hair and she fell forward, managing to catch herself by her palms even with her wrists zip-tied.

She struggled to inhale, holding herself up on all fours. Struggled to calm herself. Struggled to blink back the tears that wanted to spill over.

He wanted her screams and her tears and her pain. He wanted her to beg him to stop. He wanted to know he had all the control, and she was nothing.

She had to find some way to not give it to him. She sucked in a breath, squeezed her eyes shut. Two tears fell onto the ground beneath her. If they fell, maybe he wouldn't see them when he looked at her face again.

She stared at the two drops of moisture, willing them to be all. And that was when she really looked at the floor, the splintered chair, and the little glimpse of something shiny.

A piece of metal lying in between a gap in the floorboards. A dime. She almost sobbed right then and there. She'd stopped believing in signs from the universe, from people she'd lost a long, long time ago.

But seeing a dime had saved Thomas. Or at least, he claimed it had. He'd told her that story about not getting shot in the head, and in this moment… She wanted to believe. Believe *everything*.

It was her own sign. She would make it through this. Someone was watching after her.

And when she looked just a few inches beyond the dime stuck in the floorboard gap, her breath caught.

There was a nail. It wasn't very big and kind of rusty. The chances of it actually cutting through the zip ties were slim to none, and it was too short to be much of a weapon.

But it was sharp, and it was something.

Chapter Seventeen

Thomas drove to Fairmont at illegal speeds, sirens screeching. But once he reached the city limits, he slowed and turned off the sirens. He didn't want to scare off anyone who might work at the convenience store, and he had a few questions for Rosalie he didn't want to have to scream over the sirens to ask.

"I don't need the illegal details, but how did you manage to track down an alias? We've been trying to get information out of his friends and family and workplace since we got those photos."

"And what did every single person you guys tried to talk to have in common? They're all *men*. Dad, brothers, SWAT team. Dude doesn't have one woman in his inner circle, and I figured there's a damn good reason for it. So I searched the precinct's employee list for a woman. I called an administrative assistant, a road officer and a woman in their crime scene squad—the only three women in their entire precinct, which is *huge* by the way. Red-flag city."

It was ingenious. The men had closed ranks around one of their own, but when there was one female victim, why wouldn't there be others?

"The road officer was no help. Guess she drank the Kool-Aid," Rosalie continued as he pulled into the convenience store parking lot. "And the crime scene lady didn't get back to me, but the administrative assistant had a *lot* to say."

"When we find Vi, we'll send her flowers."

"Damn right," Rosalie said firmly, probably needing to hear that *when* as much as Thomas needed to say it. "The big breakthrough was she mentioned that one time Eric had submitted receipts for reimbursement after some SWAT trip, and she'd had to give one of them back and refuse repayment because the name on the receipt hadn't been his. He'd tried to claim it was an undercover name, but since the department hadn't approved an undercover name credit card, they refused to pay him back. He raised a big stink about it. Big enough that she remembered the other name."

Thomas pulled into a parking spot next to the store.

"I spent all night…very *legally* researching the alias." She flashed Thomas a smile that was half-hearted in its rebelliousness. "I got a credit card and *magically* got into his recent purchase history. I saw it was used here, and then… *very much* obtained security footage through the letter of the law, and here we are."

"Here we are. Thank God we've got someone who's not a cop on our side." He pushed the door open, but his phone trilling stopped him. It was a call from Copeland.

"What's the update?" Thomas answered by way of greeting.

"The ping of the postal inspector's phone is a dead end. She turned it off before she left Bent city limits. They'll keep trying. If she turns it back on, we'll have her."

He wasn't surprised, but he was disappointed. It was a big if. Clearly, she didn't want to be found.

"We did get some information this morning from poking around Fairmont. Dianne Kay had a meeting with a Realtor

Monday. Laurel's on her way over to meet with the woman and talk to her and see what she can find out."

"A Realtor?" Was the postal inspector just…planning on moving here? Was this a dead end, a great happenstance coincidence?

"I'm in Fairmont. Rosalie got me a lead I want to follow up on." He relayed everything Rosalie had told him in the office. "We're going to interview the convenience store employees. I need you to go to the postal inspector's hotel. See if Eric Carter was staying here. I'll forward you the security cam still and his alias."

"That's promising. I'll show it around. If we can prove that Eric Carter and the postal inspector are working together, we should be able to get a search warrant to ping his phone."

He'd probably have it turned off like the inspector, but it was something. A chance. Thomas was going to believe in every chance he could.

"Keep me posted," he said to Copeland, then hung up. Rosalie had gone ahead of him into the store when he'd have preferred it if she would have waited. Frowning, he moved for the door, but Rosalie was jogging out.

"The guy who was here apparently just got off shift. Parked around back." She was already jogging around the side of the building and Thomas followed.

There indeed was a guy getting into his car. "Al Jones," Rosalie shouted.

The man stopped, half in the car and half out. He looked at them both with lots of suspicion, but slowly got back out of the car. "Who's asking?"

"Thomas Hart. Bent County Sheriff's Department. I have a few questions I need to ask you."

Al studied him. "You aren't dressed like a cop."

Thomas pulled his badge out of his pocket. "I'm a detective. We have information that a man going by the name Jim Errin bought some stuff from the store Friday night."

He shrugged. "Lots of people do."

Rosalie held out the picture she had. "This guy."

To his credit, Al studied the picture with a furrowed brow. "Yeah, I remember him." He handed the picture back and said nothing else.

Thomas only resisted growling because Rosalie did it for him.

"Can you tell us what you remember? When he came in? What he did?" Thomas asked.

Al sighed. "Yeah, I guess. It was kinda early in the night. I start at nine and it was before ten for sure. He bought gas. Some food and a twelve-pack. I only remember because he complained about the price of beer. Told him if he didn't like it, go to a grocery store. Thought I was going to have to call the cops the way he looked at me. But then he just left."

It wasn't much, but it was something. "He have a woman with him? In the store or maybe waiting in the car?"

Al shook his head. "He was alone, but he bought enough snacks for two people or a long time."

"Anything else?" Rosalie demanded.

"He was definitely carrying, but that's about it. Made his little complaint, then left."

Carrying. Great.

"Which way did he go?"

"Hell if I know, lady."

Since Rosalie looked like she was about to start punching, Thomas intervened.

"Thanks for your cooperation." Thomas took a card out of his pocket. "You think of anything else, even if it seems small, give me a call."

Al took the card, eyed it. Then pocketed it. "Sure."

Thomas doubted anything would come of it, but every little lead got them something else. Maybe he couldn't prove Eric was with Dianne from this, but it was a step.

They walked back to his car, and he considered driving over to the hotel and see where Copeland was in interviewing people. He'd have to talk to the front desk and the housekeeping crew. Other residents. It was a big job, and he could help make it go faster.

But before he could even pull out of the parking lot, his phone rang again. The readout was Jack Hudson, the sheriff of Sunrise. His family also ran a cold case investigation business.

For a moment, Thomas was frozen with the gripping, terrible fear that if they didn't find something soon, Vi could become a cold case herself.

"Well, are you going to answer it?" Rosalie demanded.

Thomas managed to snap himself out of it, cleared his throat. "Hart," he answered, telling himself it would be good news. Good news only. Great news.

"Hart, Jack Hudson here. I got your email. I don't know if I have a lead for you, but I talked to one of my deputies this morning and I think I might. We had a run-in with a rental car out here this weekend."

Thomas tried not to get excited. He knew the postal inspector had been in Sunrise Saturday morning, because Vi had met with her at Coffee Klatsch.

Rosalie cleared her throat and gave him a pointed look. So he put the phone on speaker so they could both listen. "What kind of run-in?"

"We don't get a lot of visitors out this way, so it's notable to see a rental car at all. But we had one speeding around Saturday morning. One of my deputies pulled the driver over. She claimed not to know the speed limit. My deputy ended up letting her off with a warning. No big deal."

"And I'm guessing this was Postal Inspector Dianne Kay?"

"That's what her license said. Honestly, even with the information you sent me, I wouldn't have thought anything of it, but later that afternoon he got a call out at Fish 'N' Ammo. Some guy was arguing over ammo prices, and you know Vern. He'd die poor and out of spite rather than take someone's money he thought was disrespecting him. He refused to sell to the guy after that. The guy put up a stink. Vern called us. The same deputy who pulled over the inspector answered the call, but by that time, the guy had already left. When Vern gave a description of the car and a partial plate, though, it was the same car from the speeding woman."

Which connected Eric Carter and Dianne Kay. "Do me a favor, Jack, forward all reports and any information you've got on both calls to me, Laurel and Vicky in admin at Bent County."

"Sure thing. I'll get right on it, and I'll let you know if we see the car again, or any of the people in your email."

"Thanks, Jack. Appreciate it." Thomas hit End on the phone, everything inside of him humming with possibility. This wasn't going to be a cold case. They had a lead.

Laurel and Vicky would work on the search warrant for Eric's phone. But it was clear, if Eric and Dianne were sharing a rental car they had *both* been in Sunrise on Saturday. Which led him to believe, Eric wasn't in Fairmont anymore. Or at least, he had somewhere to hide near Sunrise.

Thomas turned to Rosalie. "I think we should go to Sunrise."

"Get up," Eric yelled.

Vi inched forward, pretending she was trying to push up,

but what she was really doing was inching her hand closer to the gap, to the nail. Once she was close enough, she pushed back onto her feet, then in a quick move, blocked by her body, swept her hand over the crack and managed to pick up the nail and palm it before standing.

It felt like nothing considering the pain she was in, but *positive thinking*. It *could* be something, in the right moment.

Once on her feet, she carefully did a shuffle turn to face Eric. Her entire head throbbed. Her shoulder was a dull ache. Her throat still hurt from where he'd choked her.

Part of her wanted to say something snarky. To just keep fighting back. But she knew eventually he would snap, and she'd be dead. For every day this dragged out, it was another day Thomas might find her.

Maybe he didn't know Eric was here, but he knew the postal inspector was the last person to see her. He had to know that. Between him and Laurel and Copeland, and Rosalie no doubt, they were going to find her.

So she had to stay alive, but that didn't mean she'd cower. She met Eric's dark, empty eyes, chin up, no matter how everything ached.

"Now that you ruined sitting for yourself, you can just stand." He turned to Dianne. "Clean that mess up. Then bring me a sandwich." He stalked out of the room, into a hallway that must have led to a bedroom and a bathroom.

Dianne scurried over to pick up the pieces of broken chair. Vi pretended to move out of the way, when what she was really doing was trying to hide a piece of debris that might help her.

She shuffled back, taking a small splinter or two with her, and Dianne was apparently worried enough about making that sandwich that she didn't see them. Once Dianne was in the kitchen, pulling food out of bags and a cooler, Vi just kept shuffling back until she reached the wall. She leaned against it.

She breathed until she had stilled some, until her vision calmed. Everything was going to keep throbbing no doubt, so she ignored the pain.

And focused on the nail in her hand. There was no way to bend her fingers or hands to get the nail to push against the plastic of the zip ties. She did everything she could, even as the plastic bit into her skin. But it was no use.

Okay, so that doesn't work. Doesn't mean it was pointless. She looked down at the two shards of wood, then back up at Dianne. Who now had a full sandwich on a paper plate. She didn't so much as glance Vi's way as she rushed into the hallway.

Murmured voices, a shout, but Vi couldn't pay attention to it. She crouched and picked up the pieces of chair. She examined them. One was flimsy. Any kind of pressure on it and it would snap. But the other had some decent thickness to it, though it was a little sharp.

What the hell did she think she was going to do with these sad items?

Something. I'm going to come up with something.

A crash sounded from the other room. No thuds followed, so Vi assumed Eric had just thrown something, not hit Dianne. She knew the sounds all too well.

Vi straightened, just in time for Dianne to come rushing out. She kept her back to Vi, but Vi could see the woman's shoulders shake, like she was crying. Still, it was a silent cry.

Eric didn't appreciate tears.

She started putting the food away, back to Vi.

"Are you going to knock me around if I sit on the ground?"

Dianne looked over at her with a sneer. Her eye was bloody, along with the tears, and it gave Vi a full body shudder. "I guess you'll have to risk it and see."

Which didn't feel like too big a risk considering the woman was hurt and crying, and no doubt knew she would get worse if she left a mess in the kitchen and Eric reappeared.

So carefully and slowly, Vi lowered herself to the ground, using the wall behind her as a kind of balance. With the zip ties around her ankles, she could only either keep her knees up at her chin or slide them out in front of her. Carefully, so her legs would hide the chair debris, she straightened her legs and leaned against the wall. It wasn't the most comfortable sitting position, but it was better than standing.

Dianne was sniffling in the kitchen, occasionally eating the tiniest bite of food. And Vi just…didn't understand. This woman had been a professional in a law enforcement job. Maybe Vi didn't know what her childhood had been like, but on the outside she seemed like a strong, successful woman.

And she was letting Eric knock her around. Why? Why did he just get to *do* this? What made a mean, vicious man so powerful?

It didn't make any sense. Maybe she could see why Eric had targeted her, manipulated her, but she'd been vulnerable and desperate to find something *solid*, and he'd pretended to be just that.

But this woman was none of those things. So *how*?

"Don't you want to stop this?" Vi demanded. Undeniably *angry*—not even at Dianne, but at this whole situation and that one mistake years ago had upended her entire life to bring her here. Kidnapped and injured, even after finally clawing her way out.

And now, because he'd found some new woman to manipulate and torture, she was sucked back into this hell.

But *that* woman wasn't tied up.

"You can walk right out that door. You can grab that gun and stop him. Why are you crying and *taking* it when you can get the hell out?"

Dianne stood very still, her back to Vi. And for a moment, Vi felt a surge of hope so big, so deep that tears sprang to her eyes. Maybe she could get through to Dianne. Maybe she could end this right here. Right now.

But Dianne didn't move, didn't speak, so Vi wracked her brain for the right thing to say. What would have gotten through to her if she put herself back there?

It was deflating, because she wasn't sure anything would have. She'd been so certain it was her punishment for the mistakes she'd made. It had only been saving Magnolia that had become bigger than that shame. And only after she'd gotten out did she realize none of it was her fault or her shame.

But that didn't mean she could give up on Dianne.

"I know you can do this," Vi said. "*I* did it. And it took *everything* I am." And a bigger purpose. But if she thought about Mags anymore right now, she'd just lose it. "But you're…you're in such a better position. You can take him down, Dianne. We can stop him from hurting us and other people."

"He has the bullets," she muttered. "And two more guns in there."

Which wasn't a *no*. Vi's heart was beating against her chest, almost like she'd run a marathon. "We can outsmart him," she whispered. "I know we can."

Dianne finally turned to face Vi. Her eye was bloodshot,

likely from a blow. A trickle of blood came from the corner of her mouth. But Vi didn't see any kind of *fight* in her eyes.

"He loves me," Dianne said, as if under some kind of spell. "And once this is over, I won't be getting on his nerves anymore. It'll go back to the way things were. And we'll be happy. Once you're out of the way, we'll be happy."

"Is that what he told you?" Vi shook her head, and it was impossible to keep the tears in check right now. "He doesn't. He doesn't love anyone or anything, including himself. He's broken, Dianne. And if someone can save him, it's a trained professional. *Not* us."

"I have saved him, and I will again."

"No. You won't. He won't go back to the fake guy who talked you into loving him. He didn't hit me until I was married to him, did he tell you that? We dated for almost a year, and he never once laid a hand on me. Not because of *me*. Because of *him*."

Dianne rolled her eyes. Some of that fight was coming back, but only against Vi. Not for them.

"Dianne, you do not have to live like this. You are a *postal inspector*. The cops will help us. Everyone will—"

"Just shut up, or I really will knock you around. And I'd be happy to end it all." She looked at the gun in the corner, as if considering it, even though she'd said the bullets weren't in it. "Right here, right now, not drag it out. So I can get on with my real life."

Which was enough of a threat for Vi to keep her mouth shut. And she went back to thinking about her sad little weapons and what she could possibly do with them.

Legs free, she could run. Arms free, she could fight.

Someway. Somehow. Because Dianne might still be a victim of Eric.

But Vi wouldn't be.

Chapter Eighteen

Thomas screeched to a stop in front of Sunrise's Fish 'N' Ammo, little more than a shed off the highway and in the very outskirts of Sunrise proper. He beat Rosalie to the door, but only narrowly.

There was a young man behind the counter, early twenties. Thomas didn't recognize him but supposed he couldn't know *everyone* in Bent County. "Is Vern here?"

The young man looked from Thomas to Rosalie. His eyes lingered on Rosalie. Who smiled wide and bright at the kid.

"Faster the better, sweetheart," she said with a wink.

The guy blushed, then scurried out from behind the counter. "Yeah, sure." He went into the back room and when he came out, Vern, followed.

He was a short, burly man in his late seventies who'd been running this hole-in-the-wall of a shop since Thomas could remember.

"Hart," he offered gruffly. "Ma'am."

Rosalie rolled her eyes, but she didn't say anything.

"I've got a few questions about the incident you had here with a man on Saturday."

"Out-of-towner," Vern said with a sneer. "If it ain't some dumb kid, it's some out-of-towner."

Hart nodded, trying to find some deeper well of patience left inside of him. "Sheriff told me you guys had a little argument."

"That's right. He comes in here, complains to my face, then thinks I'm going to sell to him? Fat chance. He got real agitated and I figured best if I had a deputy nearby. Had Gav here call the cops." He jerked a thumb at the kid.

Gav nodded, still looking a little lovelorn in Rosalie's direction. The Fish 'N' Ammo wasn't exactly a hot spot for young people.

"He left though. He definitely wanted a fight, but something scared him off." Vern shrugged.

"When he drove away, did you see which way he went?"

"Yeah, west into town." Vern pointed out the door. "I talked to Gladys at the diner Saturday night, and she said she saw the car speed past, so I know he went that way."

That was good information. Maybe. But west of Sunrise still wasn't a *location*. Still, he thanked Vern, handed his card to the man with instructions to call if he returned or if Vern thought of anything else.

Before Thomas and Rosalie could leave and decide their next move, a bell tinkled above the door. Jack Hudson strode in. He nodded his head at Vern, approached Thomas and Rosalie. "Hart. Rosalie. Figured this'd be your first stop. When Vern told me Gladys had seen the car too, I decided to go around and talk to the business owners along the highway and see if anyone else had seen the car. We don't get a lot of traffic all the way out here, so I figured we'd get a few mentions. And I was right." He pulled out a small spiral notebook from his front pocket, flipped a few pages.

"I can give you a list of all the people I talked to, all the places that saw him, but the most important sighting was outside the library. Dahlia, our librarian, happened to be locking up to head home. The guy flew by. She said she might not have remembered or paid much mind, even with the speeding, but he made a screeching turn at 124th Street. She was worried because the Underkirchers let their kids ride bikes up and down the road since so few people drive it."

"124th. There's nothing down that road but ranches and more ranches. It doesn't even hook up to any of the main highways, does it?"

Jack shook his head. "It's a lot of space. Some of the ranches might back up to the interstate, but he'd have to drive over their land to get there. Seems unlikely, or at least I would have had a call about property damage by now."

Thomas nodded. "So he could be holed up somewhere out along there?"

"Seems possible. I don't know what other end destination would be out that way. My deputies can start searching and canvassing, but most of the houses are a way off the street, so not a lot of eyes on the road. Not sure we'll get much, unless someone thinks they got a trespasser and, again, I'd have a call by now on that."

"I'd appreciate them asking around anyway."

Jack nodded. "I'm sure you've thought of everything, but what about bringing in the K-9 unit?"

Thomas knew Jack brought it up because his fiancée was on the unit, so it didn't grate that Jack was suggesting something Thomas had already considered. "It's too big of an area, and we don't have enough information yet. This is good, but it's still not enough for the sheriff to approve it."

"You guys follow me out to the ranch, I can hook you up with Cash. Maybe the area's too big, but I'm sure he'd be willing to give it a shot with his dogs." Cash Hudson was Jack's brother who trained dogs for a number of things, including for the sheriff's department and for search and rescue.

Thomas knew it couldn't hurt. "Okay, we'll follow you out that way."

He and Rosalie got into his patrol car and started driving out to the Hudson Ranch.

He hadn't gotten far when Laurel called. He answered the phone on speaker.

"Hart."

"I just got done harassing a real estate agent and everyone in her office. She told me what Kay was looking for—land, out of the way, outbuildings preferable but didn't need to be in good shape. She didn't want to give me specifics, but I finally got a list of the addresses she'd given to Inspector Kay."

"Are any of them out by Sunrise, on 124th Street?"

Laurel was quiet for just a second. "As a matter of fact, nearly all of them. I take it you've got a lead?"

"Yeah, send me the addresses, though. They'll narrow it down." He hoped. "Any word from Copeland?"

"No, think he's still interviewing hotel employees. I'm going to apply for search warrants on these addresses, then I'll head over and give him a hand. If we don't get anything there and nothing else crops up, we'll meet you in Sunrise. Unless you want us to come out now?"

"No. But I want to know why we don't have a search warrant to ping Eric Carter's phone yet. The evidence is there. I want it done."

"On it. Talk soon." The call ended.

No doubt Eric, or his alias, had also turned off his phone, but if they could get a ping anywhere in the Sunrise vicinity, even if it wasn't a direct hit, maybe they could narrow it down.

"That isn't a coincidence," Rosalie said, leaning forward in her seat. "It *can't* be."

"If you've got service, see if you can look up anything about the addresses she texts me."

Rosalie nodded. He followed Jack out to the Hudson Ranch, passed the main house and up to a big outbuilding that Thomas knew housed Cash's many dogs.

Cash and his wife, Carlyle, were standing outside eyeing both police cars skeptically when Jack and Thomas got out of their cars. Thomas knew all the players, because not only had he worked with all the Hudsons, but Carlyle had essentially saved Laurel's life a while back. She was the newest Delaney-Carson addition's namesake, in fact, though they called her Cary to avoid confusion.

"We've got a missing person case we're hoping you can help us with," Jack said by way of greeting.

Thomas explained the situation, doing his best to leave his personal connection and feelings out of it, but considering all the different connections, he doubted very much that Cash and Carlyle didn't *know* Vi was…his.

Cash considered the information Jack and Thomas gave him.

"I only have two dogs right now trained to do scent-specific tracking. But we can give it a shot. If you've got an idea of where you want to start, we can head out now. But we do have to get property owner approval before we do any searching. Legally, anyway."

"All three properties I want searched are up for sale. I'm working on a search warrant." But… "I don't care about legality right now. I want her found, then we can worry about the rest."

Cash nodded. "Then let's head out."

Vi HAD FIGURED that at some point Dianne and Eric would sleep and she'd be able to work on using her pathetic tools for some kind of escape chance. She was tied up. Wouldn't they think that was good enough?

Apparently not, because Dianne never left the main room. Even as the cabin had gotten pitch-black as night fell, Vi would occasionally hear Dianne do something in the kitchen, or she'd see a flash of light that was Dianne's phone screen.

Vi had used the dark time not to sleep herself—if she even could have in this uncomfortable sitting position. But she'd considered her nail, her shards of chair. She couldn't hold the nail in any way to break her bonds, but if she could somehow get the nail into the floor, sharp point upward, she could use her bodyweight to push plastic against sharp point.

She'd figured out it would take more than one puncture to get herself free of the zip tie, so it would take time. But it was possible. If she could manage to get the nail upright and sturdy.

By the time daylight started illuminating the cabin, Vi had an idea. But it'd have to wait until Dianne wasn't quite so close.

The woman in question was hard at work in the kitchen, clearly trying to put together some kind of breakfast feast for Eric.

Vi almost pointed out the futility. She was sure he would find something wrong with it, and if Dianne wanted to listen, she could predict, with dizzying accuracy, just what he'd say was wrong.

Rubbery eggs. Cold toast. Slimy bacon. It didn't matter if any of those things were true. It wasn't about *truth*. It was about power. It had taken Vi too long, and a lot of space away from Eric, to be able to learn that.

But since she *had* learned it, she went ahead and told Dianne exactly that. Why not? Dianne would have to find the bullets to do anything about it.

Besides, maybe just maybe, one of these times, she could get through to Dianne. Poke enough holes in her theory of *love* and show Dianne how wrong she was. How wrong this *all* was.

"He'll eat his fill, then throw the plate at the wall and tell you all the ways it's trash. Because it doesn't matter if you can cook or not, Dianne. It doesn't matter how hard you slaved away at it. He just wants to make you feel bad."

Dianne pretended not to hear, and marched off down the hallway, plate heaped with food in her hands.

Vi figured she had *maybe* five minutes of being alone. So she got to work. Carefully, meticulously, she balanced the nail on its head next to her on the ground.

Then, she scooted onto her knees. She took the skinniest shard of chair and carefully positioned it over the sharp point of the nail, with the nail in the center. Since the wood wasn't sturdy, it only took pushing down with her bodyweight for the nail to pierce the wood.

It wasn't as stable as she would have liked, the wood splintering a bit on impact, but it was something. If she could stabilize the wood with her knees, she now had a somewhat unmovable sharp point that would allow her to do the same thing with her zip tie that she'd just done with the splinter.

Push the zip tie against the sharp point, using her bodyweight as some kind of lever to pierce. Through the plastic. She just needed to find the right way to arrange her body so that she didn't actually impale her hands *with* the nail.

Luckily, it wasn't a long nail, so whatever damage she

ended up doing to herself would likely be minimal. What was some tetanus if she managed to get freedom?

She nudged the wood under her knees, managed to get them close enough together that her own bodyweight held the wood, and thus the nail, still.

She gave one furtive look down the hall. No sound yet. No yelling. She still had time. She placed part of the plastic zip tie on top of the sharp nail, then used her bodyweight to push down.

For a moment, nothing happened, then she fell forward. She looked at the plastic and nearly laughed out loud.

It worked. It *worked*.

It didn't actually get her hands unbound yet, but there was now a tiny hole in the plastic. With enough tiny holes, the plastic would break. And her hands would be free and…

She eyed the gun on the kitchen corner. Well, she'd have to get over there with her feet still tied. She'd have to find bullets.

But it was something. Chances. Opportunities. If she was smart. If she was careful. Everything could…

There was no yelling. No crash. But Vi heard footsteps getting closer so she quickly moved back onto her butt, and hid the nail and chair shard under her legs.

Dianne returned with an empty plate and a smirk. Like she'd won some contest.

Woo-hoo, he didn't hit you this time. Congratulations.

Eric appeared just a few seconds later. His hair was wet, like maybe he'd showered. He was wearing new clothes. He was whistling as he came out of the hallway, but he stopped short when he saw Dianne put the plate in the sink.

Then move away.

Vi closed her eyes. She knew what came next.

"What the hell do you think you're doing?" Eric demanded in a cold, distant voice.

Dianne stopped on a dime, freezing with eyes wide. "I was just going to…to eat my…"

"Eat? You were going to leave this mess and *eat*?" He didn't storm over to her. He moved with a quiet kind of stealth that no doubt made him good at his job. All menacing force in the quietest of moves.

Even Vi found herself holding her breath as he advanced on Dianne, towered over her as she hunched down and looked away.

"I'm so—"

Before she could finish the word, Eric's hands were around her throat. She made terrible noises as he squeezed. She fought him. Kicked and scratched out, her eyes getting wider and wider until Vi had to look away. Squeeze her eyes shut.

"You eat when I tell you to," he said, his voice low and cold. "You clean up when you make a mess or you are *useless* to me. Do you hear me?"

But Dianne obviously said nothing, because he had his hands around her throat still. Vi didn't want to look, but it wasn't *stopping*. So she did.

"Eric, you're going to kill her," Vi said, knowing it was pointless. Knowing there was nothing to be done. He either didn't hear her or just didn't care. He just kept squeezing as Dianne's fight got jerkier and less… Just *less*.

He didn't look away. And when he finally dropped Dianne, she didn't move. She just crumpled onto the floor in a heap.

Vi was shaking, trying to breathe without making noise. But he was coming for her now, and no matter how hard she tried to hold on to her strength, her hope, her determination, fear won.

He rolled back his sleeves, looked down at her with that pleasant smile that was only ever a lie. "Now it's your turn."

Chapter Nineteen

In the end, they split the three addresses between them.

Cash took Rosalie and a dog to the one closest to Sunrise and one of Jack's deputies was going to meet them for a police presence. The online listing Rosalie had found showed that the sale was really more for the property rather than any of the buildings, though there was a barn still in good shape.

Carlyle went with Jack and a dog to the one farthest down 124th. This property had no pictures on its listing and was definitely just about the land. The description listed some "rustic" buildings that could easily be razed by someone with a "creative plan" for the acreage.

Thomas and another Hudson brother, Palmer, went to the address sort of in the middle of the other two. The thought being if the dogs on either end found something, Thomas could get to either of the other properties quickly and involve Bent County if necessary.

The property he was driving to had included a house and pictures in the listing. A little small, a lot old. Definitely not something someone would buy if they were looking to move into it in the near future.

All three listings gave Thomas hope they were on the right track. Why was the postal inspector looking at land for sale with no houses, no signs of life, if she wasn't looking for a place to hide? And if she'd found one, now Thomas would find her.

And Vi. *Please God, let me find Vi.*

Thomas drove his patrol car down the street with Palmer in the passenger seat. They'd brought a dog with them too, sitting happily in the back, but it wasn't trained for scent-specific tracking. Cash had explained the difference, but Thomas hadn't been paying much attention at that point. He'd been looking at the property listings.

In the end, he got the gist. The two with Cash and Carlyle could track Vi's specific scent. This one could only alert him to human presence, not Vi specifically.

The scent-specific dogs would search for Vi thanks to a scrunchie Rosalie had in her purse that Vi had last used, and Thomas's bag because it had been in the same house Vi had last been at.

The dog in his back seat was more search and rescue, on the scent for *any* body. Cash had warned that hits with any of the dogs were a pretty big reach considering the sheer area they had to case, but he'd also seen no reason not to try.

And with the addresses narrowing things down, Thomas hoped there was more of a chance.

"Right there," Palmer said, pointing at an entrance off the highway Thomas probably would have missed. It was covered in over brush, but they could see a green sign with the property number amid the brush. And it wasn't *totally* overgrown. Someone had driven through here recently.

Probably in an attempt to sell the place, take the pictures on the listing, etc. The photographer had certainly avoided certain parts of the property. Like the overgrown entrance, the barely-there gravel on the gravel road that would lead to the house.

He followed the road at a slower pace, watching the world around them. Mountains in the distance, and overgrown, poorly kept ranch land around them. Thomas kept an eye open for *any* thing that pointed to *people*.

But it was all so damn abandoned. He thought something in the distance was maybe the house, but in the end, it had just been a pile of trash. A rusted-out car, old appliances, rusty ranch equipment that had no doubt been left to the elements at least a decade ago, if all the overgrowth obscuring half the trash was anything to go by.

And still the gravel road went on, the house not coming into view until they'd been driving a good ten minutes. It felt like the deadest of dead ends, but Thomas didn't say that. They had to check into every possibility. That was why he was lucky to have so many people helping. All over Bent County, people were working to find Vi.

He tried to have that be the central anchor of faith he held on to. Because he'd worked a lot of hopeless cases and found hope somewhere along the way. He'd done what felt impossible, time and time again, so why shouldn't he believe the same was possible *here*? When it mattered to him most.

He couldn't give up hope on Vi.

He stopped his car in front of the house and got out. Palmer got out on his side, then let the dog out. He gave the dog whatever orders it needed, and the dog got to work.

Though the *work* looked a lot like running around.

Thomas moved for the house, hand on the butt of his gun in its holster on his hip. He did a quick perimeter check, then carefully walked up one of the porches. He tried to look in windows, but most were grimy or covered with curtains.

The knob had one of those Realtor lockboxes on it. He

could get the bolt cutters out of his trunk and take care of it. Maybe he would, but… He looked out at the dog, who sniffed the porches, and different trees. But everything seemed heavily deserted, and even the dog didn't alert to *any* sign of human life.

Thomas went to the back door, jiggled the knob there, then listened with his ear on the door. But he heard a whole lot of nothing.

Palmer came to stand at the bottom of the stairs of the porch Thomas stood on. He gestured at the dog, bounding through the tall grass of the side yard.

"He's not coming up with anything," Palmer said. "Except squirrels. I can send him out into the woods, but…"

"Seems like a waste of time," Thomas finished for him.

Palmer nodded. "If someone had been around here in the past few days, even if they hadn't been in the house, the dog should come up with something." He shoved his hands into his pockets. "I can have the dog trail the car back up to the highway, see if he sniffs anything along the road. I doubt he'll come up with anything, but you'll feel better if we cover every base."

Thomas blew out a breath. It was the death of any case. Focusing so much on tiny details you missed the big picture—or being so obsessed with the big picture, you missed the details. You had to find a middle ground, and Palmer's idea was probably it.

"All right."

Palmer called the dog, gave him some more orders as Thomas climbed in the driver's seat.

"You don't have to drive slow enough for him to keep up, just slow enough he can keep us in sight," Palmer said as he took his seat. Thomas nodded and Palmer rolled down the window and Thomas drove.

Impatience bit at him. Hopefully the other two groups were having better luck, but what if they weren't? They were reaching a second night of her being gone. Every minute was a chance something bad could happen to her, and he was driving around damn dead ends.

Not dead ends. Lead after tiny lead. But there was a war inside him. Between a detective who knew what to do, and a man desperate to save the woman he loved.

They were not compatible.

About halfway back up the road, Thomas's phone started pinging, and he realized they'd been out of cell range. He steered with one hand, pulled his phone out of his pocket with the other. He had texts and voice messages coming in. He started with the messages. The first one was from Jack.

"We've got something," Jack said. "We haven't even let the dog out because there's a run-down cabin with a car out front. The rental car."

Thomas didn't even bother to listen to the rest. He just tossed his phone down, slammed on the brakes.

"Get the dog," he ordered Palmer, who was already half-way out the door. When Palmer got back in the car with the dog, Thomas put both hands on the wheel and hit the gas pedal. Hard.

VI'S KEEP-A-STIFF-UPPER-LIP MANTRA was slowly fading. Because she was almost certain Dianne was dead. *Dead.* Eric had just strangled her like she was *nothing*, and it left Vi feeling…alone or less protected. Even though Dianne had been working against her, she'd been a hope. She'd been a distraction to Eric. She'd been *something*.

Now it was just Vi and her ex-husband. Who'd just *killed* someone. Someone he thought he loved. Or had thought loved him. Vi didn't even know anymore. She just knew she had to get out of here.

"I thought you were going to draw this out, not kill me," Vi managed to say, but her voice shook. And Eric grinned. It made her want to throw up.

"I don't think she's dead." He looked back at Dianne's lifeless body. Shrugged. "Or she is. But you're right. I've got plans for you before I kill you." His eyes moved over her whole body, until death seemed a better alternative than what she had a horrible feeling he was thinking about.

He put his hand on his belt, laughed when she followed the move with her eyes, no doubt fear and terror evident on every last inch of her face.

"Oh, come on, Vi. You always liked it."

Vi had to breathe through the terror, the utter panic. How would she fight him off? Kicking and fighting hadn't worked for Dianne, and she'd had all her limbs free.

What was she going to—

The silence in the room was interrupted by something outside. A kind of... A dog was barking outside. Vi held her breath. *Please. Please. Please.*

"What the hell is that?" he muttered. "No one should be around here for miles." He moved back into the kitchen, with absolutely no regard for Dianne's body on the floor. He grabbed his gun, then disappeared into the hallway. Probably getting those bullets Dianne had mentioned were in the bedroom.

He returned, loading the gun as he walked. He didn't even look at Vi. Just went to the front door and disappeared outside.

Vi wanted the dog barking to be some kind of sign, some kind of *help*...well, as long as Eric didn't end up shooting the help. But she also knew it didn't matter what happened out there. On the chance Eric came back and the dog barking meant nothing, she had to be free.

She got her tiny board from under her legs and positioned it under her knees again. She realized she was crying when the tears fell off her cheeks and landed with a *plop* on the wood.

She ignored it all and got to work. Pushing the plastic of the zip tie against the sharp tip of the nail over and over again, as many times as she could, making as many holes as she could.

Maybe he'd come in and catch her. She didn't care. Dianne still hadn't so much as moved or made a sound. God, she had to be dead.

It wasn't going to be Vi. She wouldn't let it be her. She wouldn't let herself be a victim for one more second. She wouldn't abandon her child. She wouldn't lose a future with Thomas. A future for *herself.*

But the door flew open. Vi scrambled to hide her lone hope for escape.

"Someone let their damn dogs run loose," Eric was grumbling. "Stupid country hicks." He kicked the door shut with his leg. He marched back to the kitchen, without even looking at Vi, so she was able to keep subtly moving her board under her legs.

Eric leaned the gun in the corner, then reached down and grabbed Dianne's lifeless body.

He dragged her body over the floor. She was nothing but limp limbs. Vi wanted to look away, but something kept her glued to the morbid sight.

He shoved the body against the door. A human block. "There. Let anyone get past *that*," he said, oh-so-pleased with himself.

But Vi could only stare at Dianne. Was she hallucinating or was there still the faint rise and fall of Dianne's chest?

"Now you. You can't be anywhere near these windows until I know for sure no one's lurking around out there."

Vi tried to think clearly as he came for her. This was better than what he'd been planning just a few minutes ago. She hoped.

He grabbed around the zip tie on her ankles and began to drag her. The plastic dug through her pants and into her skin. She tried to hold back the whimper and the sting of pain, the rough scrape of floor against her back, the bruised shoulder blade from yesterday.

But she *did* whimper, and he laughed and laughed all the way to a door in the kitchen. He opened it with another loud slam. Inside the dim closet was an array of shelves and some random kitchen items. A broom, a mousetrap, some canned goods. It was some kind of pantry.

He'd dragged her as far as he could from her feet, but she still wasn't fully in the pantry. So he started using the boot of his heel to push her body into the pantry. Then he kicked her once, luckily on a more padded part of her leg so it didn't hurt as much as he'd probably like. But she got the hint. She pulled her leg in so that she was completely in the pantry.

"Sit tight. We'll have fun later." Then he slammed the door. The closet was completely and utterly dark. She couldn't see. She couldn't do anything to free her legs. The doorknob jiggled, so he must be doing something to lock her in here.

But she had put a lot of holes in the zip ties around her wrist. If she could find something in the closet to hook around the tie and then use her bodyweight to pull and put enough force on it, it might break where she'd weakened it.

And then her hands would be free. Which wasn't *much*, but if Eric left that gun loaded, and in the kitchen, just a few steps from this pantry door...all she had to do was get out, grab the gun, shoot.

But none of it mattered unless she broke these zip ties, so she set out to do just that.

Chapter Twenty

Thomas arrived at the address Jack and Carlyle had originally taken to search. It was a lot like the one he'd just been at. A kind of overgrown entrance, and Thomas really would have missed this one if not for Jack's patrol car parked out front, half in the ditch since there was no shoulder along the road here. Jack and Carlyle were standing in the ditch.

Thomas pulled up behind him and was already getting out of the car even *as* he pushed it into Park.

Jack wasted no time to explain the situation.

"Like I said in the message, we got here and did a quick canvass. The rental car that my deputy pulled over this weekend was parked behind the... Well, it's kind to call it a house anymore. After I left you that message, we let the dog out, just to see if she'd get a hit for Vi specifically. The dog alerted that she smelled Vi with a bark."

Thomas didn't like that. A bark could alert those inside of police presence, especially someone like Eric who *was* police, and could have experience with K-9s and how they worked.

"We had a visual on the door, but kept out of sight," Jack continued. "A man fitting Eric Carter's description came out. He was carrying a gun—semiautomatic. He didn't see us or the dog, as we'd called her back. He scanned the yard, then went back inside. I don't think he suspects police, but you never know."

Thomas was already itching to move, but Jack was still talking.

"We've called Sunrise and Bent County for backup. Sunrise should be here in ten minutes, tops. Bent might be a few more with the regional SWAT team."

Thomas shook his head. "No SWAT."

"This is, essentially, a hostage situation," Jack said pointedly. Like Thomas might not have the most objective handle on the situation.

And he didn't, but... "Yeah, and I know how to handle a hostage situation."

"But maybe you shouldn't handle it in this case," Jack said.

Thomas looked from Jack, to Palmer, to Carlyle. He'd worked in some capacity with each of them over the past few years. When he and Jack had been deputies at Bent County. Then with Hudson Sibling Solutions, their cold case investigative business, and then over the past year with dangerous situations that had cropped up with their family.

And not *once* had they backed off when people they cared about were in trouble.

So Thomas didn't even bother to tell Jack he was wrong. He just kept talking, like Jack had never voiced an objection. "We have a volatile criminal who is trained SWAT— hence why I don't want them going in there. He knows their moves, the training. It isn't safe," Thomas said. "We have a postal inspector we don't know much about likely in there unless they have a second vehicle. Seems unlikely. She's *also* trained law enforcement, though, and we have to keep that in mind. Likely also inside we have the..." He couldn't use the word *victim*. "...kidnapped subject, Vi Reynolds, who at the very most, knows how to shoot a gun because her cousin taught her how."

Thomas tried to hold on to that thought. Vi had learned how to protect herself some, so there was hope. He had to hold on to hope.

"You need to draw the bad guys out," Carlyle said. She held the dog by the collar, but her gaze was on the entrance with a frown.

"That would be ideal, but we have to make sure they come out of their own accord. And that they leave Vi safely out of range."

"I have an idea," Jack said. "This happened on a case a while back. A car fire was used as a distraction to draw people out. It worked pretty well then. So, what if we set a fire in their car? Maybe they'll come out to try and stop it or get anything out of the car they might have left in there. If they're concerned enough about the property, they might leave Vi in the house."

"Destruction of property? That doesn't sound like you, brother," Palmer said, at almost the same time Carlyle rubbed her hands together and said, "Ooh, I'll do it!"

"*Can* you do it?" Jack asked.

"Of course," Carlyle said with a shrug. "I'll need five minutes. Tops."

"All right," Thomas said. Maybe it wasn't the best plan, but it was a plan. Better than letting SWAT take a crack at it. "Jack, do you know anything about the property?"

"Not really any more than the listing told us."

Thomas nodded. "We'll need to surround the house best we can before Carlyle starts the distraction. At the very least cover any exit points."

"I can follow this fence on the other side down the property line, past the house a ways, then jump the fence and come in from the rear," Jack said, gesturing at the dilapidated line of wooden fence along that marked the edge of the property.

"Okay, I'll find some cover and try to get eyes on the front…"

A car crested the rise. A Bent County patrol car. And not far behind it, a Sunrise one. Both cars parked behind Thomas's, then got out. Bent County was Laurel and Copeland. Sunrise was a deputy by the name of Clinton.

"We were already on the way when we heard Jack's call go out over the radio," Laurel said as she approached. "What's the situation, the plan?" she asked and looked right at him. She didn't suggest he might not be involved, or someone else might take over.

It gave Thomas the slightest amount of relief that he wasn't doing the wrong thing by refusing to step aside.

Thomas filled them all in. Laid out the plan. They'd all spread out around the house, out of sight as much as possible at first. As more police came, they could fill in gaps. Once they had a good presence, Carlyle would start the distraction.

Ideally, it was that easy. Eric and Dianne emerged to stop the fire and were instead immediately arrested.

When another car came up, Carlyle scooted closer to the entrance. "Uh-oh, that's Cash. I better get in there before he tries to stop me. I'll draw it out. Someone signal me when you're ready for the blaze." Before anyone could agree or argue with her, she jogged off, through the entrance.

Cash pulled up behind the Sunrise patrol car. He got out and walked over with a scowl. Rosalie hurrying up behind him.

"Where exactly is my wife?" Cash demanded, like he already knew.

Palmer and Jack exchanged looks and then rocked back on their heels. "Well…"

"Setting up a distraction," Thomas supplied.

"She's going to be the death of me," Cash muttered.

"You're the one who fell in love with her," Palmer returned.

Cash only grunted. "I'm going to load up the dogs to get them out of the way, unless you think you'll need them?"

Thomas shook his head. "No, I don't think so. Best to handle this from long range."

Cash nodded, then whistled for the dog that had been with Carlyle, and let the one in Thomas's car out. So Thomas focused on the task at hand.

He had a small group of trained law enforcement. They could do this. "We spread out and surround the house. We surround, then approach, hoping the distraction lures Eric Carter and Dianne Kay out. As more cops get here, we add them to the mix. Eric Carter is our number one target. Dianne Kay is an accomplice." Thomas turned to the Sunrise deputy. "Make sure you know who's who."

"I've read the descriptions of everyone."

Thomas nodded. "Rosalie…" She wasn't going to like this. "I need someone to stay here and—"

"Bite me, Hart," she said. "I've got a gun I'm licensed to use, and like hell I'm going to stay here when you've got two civilians who can."

"I'm not exactly a civilian," Palmer said with a frown. Then sighed when that earned him quite a few sharp looks. "Fine, I'll stay here and coordinate. Make sure any new officers know the players and descriptions, then send them out to plug holes."

Thomas nodded, then looked around. A decent police presence. A lead. More officers on their way.

Vi wasn't spending another night out there.

Vi MANAGED TO hook the zip tie around her wrists on the doorknob. She carefully pulled down. She couldn't position the weaker part of the plastic exactly where she wanted it, but there was no other option that she could find here in the dark.

So, she pulled. Then leaned forward so most of her bodyweight was pulling against the plastic. The bonds bit against her skin, but she was so scared and desperate, she barely even noticed the pain.

She heard a creak, like the wood of the door splintered, and she was about to scramble up so she didn't break the damn knob off, but she heard a *snap*.

And her hands fell apart.

Apart. For a singular, shocking moment she just stood stock-still and *breathed*. Then slowly she lifted her hands up, moved her arms apart.

She'd *done* it.

She wanted to crumple to the ground and sob, but this was hardly a war won. This was one tiny battle and there were quite a few to go. She inhaled deeply, let it out and tried to decide what to do now.

Her ankles were still tied, and she didn't know how to change that without something sharp enough to cut the plastic. There might be something that sharp in this pantry, but she'd already felt around on the floor and shelves and hadn't found anything here in the dark.

She could shuffle a little with her ankles tied, but she could hardly attack or run. But if someone was out there… She didn't know where Dianne had brought her except out of town. South out of town. Would dogs really just be running around without owners? Didn't that mean there had to be neighbors or something?

Or someone coming to find her. She sat with that feeling, the horrible, overwhelming tide of hope. But if she let it infiltrate, she'd just wait. Wait for help, wait on hope, and what if it wasn't anybody?

She couldn't hope. She had to fight.

She reached out, slid her hands along the wall in front of her until she found the doorknob again. She tested it. It was locked, of course, but she could maybe fling herself at the door enough times to break it open based on the way the door had splintered when she'd used the knob, but that would make too much noise, draw too much attention.

Unless Eric was outside the cabin searching for people snooping around… Could she take that chance?

She pressed her ear against the door and listened. For a door to open, for footsteps on the porch stairs. For anything.

Just when she was about convinced that he'd left, because the house was just too still and silent, she heard the distinct sound of a shotgun being pumped.

She knew that sound, because he'd once done it a few times in front of her to scare her.

So he was still inside. She was stuck here until she heard him leave. He would leave, wouldn't he? Or was he just going to sit around with a loaded gun and wait?

It didn't matter. She couldn't worry either way. She had to set herself up for every chance, every possibility of survival. She touched the doorknob, trying to discern what kind of lock held it closed.

She could detect the tiny hole in the middle of the knob, like it was one of those Thomas had in his house where you only had to stick the little key—which was just a straight piece of metal—into the hole and then get it to catch on the mechanism inside, turn and it would unlock.

She put everything out of her mind except moving around the pantry, painstakingly slowly with her little shuffle, running her hands over every shelf. She felt cans, boxes, bags. Her fingers drifted over what were no doubt dead bugs, among other unpleasant things she wouldn't let herself think about.

God only knew how long it took. It could have been minutes or hours—she had no sense of time in the dark. In her focus.

She inhaled sharply as a slice of pain went through her finger. Damn it. She'd given herself a splinter. She couldn't *see* it, but she could feel a little sliver of wood in her finger. Of course that pain had nothing on what Eric could inflict, but it… It gave her an idea.

Could she find a splinter of wood small enough but strong enough to shove it into the keyhole of the door and undo the lock mechanism?

She carefully moved her fingers back over the wood shelf until she thought she was at the place she'd gotten a splinter. She felt around with her nails, trying to find a loose place in the wood that she could peel back and break off a chunk.

She pulled a piece off, shuffled over to the door, realized immediately it was too short and too flimsy to get the job done. So the next time she did it, she broke off multiple pieces, trying to make them thicker, sturdier, longer.

She didn't let herself think beyond that. She ignored the splinters she was getting, the pain, the fatigue. She didn't even listen for Eric. Nothing mattered right now except finding a way to unlock that door.

She was shaking by the time she got to a piece she thought might work. She was dizzy, even in the dark. No doubt because she hadn't eaten or slept, *and* she'd been knocked around. She probably didn't have much left in her if she didn't get out of this soon.

She bit down on her lip, hard, to focus. She worked tediously to get the piece of wood splinter in the keyhole, to find the right place. It took multiple tries, nearly sobbing in frustration and giving up and breaking all the sticks into a bunch of tiny pieces.

But she thought of Magnolia, and her cousins, and the possibility that Thomas was out there even now trying to save her, and she gave it another try.

Then another.

And another. Until finally it *felt* like something gave inside the knob.

She was shaking again, and nothing seemed to stop it. She worked hard to give the knob a careful test, just to see if it would turn.

It turned completely. She didn't push it open yet, though, and carefully let it go. She blew out a shaky breath, then moved back to the shelves. She grabbed the two heaviest cans she could find. Her shaking made them hard to hold, but if she could use them as weapons, she would.

She went back to the door, sucked in a steadying breath. She tucked one of the cans underneath her armpit, leaving one free to open the door. But before she could even reach out to feel for the knob, a gunshot exploded outside the door.

Far, far too close.

Chapter Twenty-One

The flames were jumping from the car's hood. Dark smoke billowed upward. There was absolutely no movement from the house.

Thomas waited, hidden behind a pole that had maybe once been some kind of security light for the property. It undoubtedly no longer worked, but it was big and bulky enough to hide him from view of the house.

Unfortunately, as time ticked by, he was coming to the conclusion that the distraction hadn't worked.

He should wait, he knew. He was by far the closest to the house—everyone else having to spread out farther to remain hidden. He should reconvene. Replan.

But damn it, the sun was starting to set and he was done with this.

He wasn't waiting any longer. He was moving in. It was an impulsive decision, but not a bad one. Not fully, anyway. And he wasn't so reckless as to not take a minute to text Laurel what he was doing and instruct her to redistribute everyone to support him.

He didn't wait for her response. He knew she wouldn't like it. He just started to move forward. Gun drawn, trying to stay low. He kept the burning car between him and the house as long as he could.

Once he'd reached that point, he sucked in a breath and

crept into the open. Anyone inside the house could see him now if they were looking out the windows, but the windows were covered in curtains.

Thomas watched them as he approached, looking for any sign of movement or life—a warning that he'd need to get down or run.

But the house seemed perfectly, utterly, *deathly* still.

He carefully moved up the front steps, trying to avoid rotting wood and places that would creak. It wasn't as quiet as he had hoped, but no one stormed out, and nothing seemed to be going on inside.

His heart sank for a moment. What if no one was inside? What if they'd gotten another car and gone to a second location? What if—

He didn't let his mind finish that what-if. He reached out for the front door and turned the handle. It gave, surprisingly, but when he tried to ease the door open, the door didn't budge. Something was blocking it.

He swore inwardly, then moved back off the porch. But he didn't go back to his hiding place like Laurel would have no doubt preferred. Instead, he began creeping around the side of the house.

There were no windows here, so he wasn't quite as worried about being caught. He paused as he reached the back of the house, being careful to come around the corner without stepping into an ambush.

But the backyard—overgrown and full of trash—seemed to be empty. Wind rustled in the towering grasses. Thomas could make out a back porch and a back door. The porch was covered in wild vines, but the door itself looked cleared, like it had been used recently.

Thomas took a breath, shoved every *emotion* out of his

mind, and focused on what needed to be done. Finding out who or what was inside that house.

Using as much cover as possible, he moved around the porch to a place that looked like he could enter. He studied the back door again—it had a small window, but it was covered by a curtain, so Thomas couldn't see inside. As silently as possible, he moved up the warped, splintered stairs of the porch to the door.

He was about to reach out, test the knob, when something flashed in the sunlight right at his foot.

A dime.

It seemed like the world around him went completely silent. And he did what he'd done all those years ago when he'd narrowly avoided a head shot.

Slower, this time, with more awareness, he bent down to pick it up—and almost immediately the glass of the door exploded. A bullet slammed into the post of the porch.

Just behind where his head had once been.

Thomas looked at the door. He couldn't shoot back. He didn't know what was going on inside. Where Vi might be if she was in there. And he could hardly stay where he was, because if the shooter had shot out through the glass, they were only going to keep shooting.

As if to prove his point, another shot went off echoing in the yard around them.

"Come any closer and she's dead," a man's voice called out. "You shoot, she's dead."

"Drop your weapon," Thomas called out, ignoring the ice that centered in his gut. He could hear everyone else coming closer. "You're surrounded. Drop your weapon and—"

The man's gun went off again, and this time Thomas knew he hadn't been quite so lucky. Pain sliced into his left arm and knocked him back a step or two, but he didn't let it knock him down.

He gritted his teeth, and against everyone yelling at him not to, charged forward.

AFTER THE SECOND SHOT, Vi figured it was now or never. Eric had to be shooting at *something*, and maybe it was dangerous to jump into a situation without being able to see what was going on, but Vi couldn't take it anymore.

She flung the pantry door open, hoping it would cause enough of a surprise that she could do *something*.

And since Eric was essentially *right there*, the barrel of his gun poised in the broken glass of the back door's window, she *could* in fact, do something.

She bashed the heavy can of food as hard as she could against his head—it would have been the back of his head, but he'd turned at the sound of the pantry door opening and it hit him right in the temple.

He crumpled, the gun clattering on top of him and then the can too, when she dropped it. For a second, she just stood there frozen while Eric groaned. It was when he began to move that she scrambled into action.

Gun first, was all she could think. She grabbed it, but so did Eric. He had a hand on the grip, and she had a hand on the barrel, which was terrible positioning. So she jerked it as hard as she could, and nearly toppled backward when it came as easily as it did.

She scurried to turn the gun around, to get her fingers on the trigger, to point it at *him*. She was shaking, damn it, she was shaking so hard. But she would shoot him if she had to. She *would*.

"You *wouldn't*," Eric seethed. He'd gotten onto all fours.

Blood poured out of a gash on his head. But he was alert. He was moving. She hadn't won yet.

She checked the gun to make sure if she pulled the trigger it would shoot. She didn't know much about shotguns, but she thought she had it right.

The back door splintered open at the same time the front door did. For a moment, Vi was *almost* distracted enough to look away, but Eric sort of lunged.

She pulled the trigger without any thought to aim or anything other than stopping that lunge. The gun exploded as his body barreled into her legs and she fell backward, narrowly missing hitting her head on the floor.

She kicked away, holding on to the gun for dear life, scrambling back and away, and it took until she was free of his weight to realize Eric wasn't fighting. He was utterly still. Blood oozed not just out of his head, but out of his shoulder now as well.

Everything went to chaos then. Both front and back doors crashed fully open, and Thomas charged through the back, his gun drawn. He was kneeling next to her in a flash, helping her to her feet.

"Vi. Are you—"

"You're bleeding. Thomas. Oh my God." There were rivulets of blood going down his left arm. She reached out as if to do something about it, but she didn't know what.

But Thomas was looking beyond her. At the body a uniformed sheriff's deputy was crouched over.

"He killed her," Vi managed to whisper. "Choked her. I thought maybe she was still breathing at one point, but..."

Thomas's gaze moved back to her. "It's all right," he soothed. She held on to that gaze, the blue, steady gaze of the man she loved.

Because she'd survived.

"Ambulances are on their way. You're all going to need one," Laurel announced grimly.

"Is he...still alive?" Vi managed to ask, though her gaze never left Thomas.

"For now. Let's focus on getting you out of here. Both of you." Laurel looked at the front door, then the back. Both with lifeless bodies. She grimaced but nodded for the front. "This way."

It wasn't lost on Vi that even while his arm bled and bled and *bled*, he was trying to shield her from seeing Dianne's body again. But she saw it.

Dead. No doubt dead.

But *she* wasn't. Somehow, Vi had survived this. This awful thing. She let Thomas lead her outside, surprised to find it almost pitch-black, with only spotlights from police cars in different areas that allowed her to see what was going on.

She could hear sirens in the distance. Ambulances. Thomas needed one. Hell, she probably needed one, but...

She turned to Thomas, and she wanted to crumple, but she didn't let herself. She did let herself lean though. She leaned her forehead into his chest. "You found me."

He held on to her with his not-shot arm. "I may never let you out of my sight again. Vi, I am so so—"

She pulled back. Fast enough it hurt him and her, and she'd be sorry about it later. But for right now? "No sorrys. There was no way of guessing Dianne was mixed up with Eric." But she saw the expression on his face. She had a feeling it would take a while to convince him of it.

But she *would*. She *would*. Because this was over.

Somehow, she'd survived. Because she'd believed she would, because she'd found her strength and fought, because she'd believed in him.

And now it was over. Really over. The kind of over that meant they got to live their lives without fear. Without envelopes showing up or having to worry.

If Eric lived, he'd go to jail for Dianne's murder. She'd testify a million times over to make sure of it.

And if he didn't...

Well, then she'd live in peace knowing she'd finally fought for herself.

Chapter Twenty-Two

Thomas was furious.

First, the paramedics had insisted on splitting them up. They'd determined Thomas needed to ride in the ambulance but let Laurel drive Vi to the hospital. Thomas would have told them to go to hell, but Laurel took over and Copeland restrained him.

Okay, not his finest moment. He'd ridden in an ambulance with a very dead Dianne Kay, while Copeland and Jack Hudson had ridden in an ambulance to watch over Eric Carter.

Thomas had been admitted to the hospital, poked and prodded, all of his demands and questions ignored. When he tried to refuse surgery, one of the nurses—whom he'd gone to high school with—told him to shut up.

He supposed it knocked some sense into him. And since Laurel was able to come update him on everything before the surgery, he supposed that helped too.

Well, except for the part where she told him Vi was getting cleared to be discharged.

"She was injured." He could see it all too clearly. The bruises on her face, her neck. And God knew what else that monster had done to her. She might have said no sorrys, but he didn't know how he wasn't supposed to feel responsible for that.

"Yes, and they've checked her out," Laurel said evenly. "She can go home and recover there. With her daughter and lots of help and love and attention from her cousins."

That's not her home anymore. But Thomas didn't know what... She'd said no sorrys, but how could some of this not be his own damn fault?

"Dianne Kay was dead on arrival," Laurel continued while the nurses prepped him for surgery. Apparently the doctor thought the bullet had fractured a bone. "Eric Carter is still in surgery. He might live. He might not. If he does, he'll go away for the rest of his life. He can't weasel his way out of this one, even if the whole state of Virginia vouched for him. Now, I need you to be a good boy and get your surgery. Maybe I'll bring you a present if you don't cry."

He glared at her, but also knew she was just trying to lighten the tension banded inside of him.

"They're not going to let her in to see you before you go, so just... Stop being a jerk and let the medical professionals do their job. When you wake up, you'll be able to see her."

If she wanted to see him. But that at least was up to Vi. He sighed. "Fine," he muttered.

And he did as he was told. So much so that the last thing he really remembered was Laurel telling him to stop being a jerk. When he woke up, he was groggy, not really sure what had happened.

It took a while to really come to, to remember, to hear what the voices in his room were saying.

"Tata!" He managed to get his eyes opened, focused. Vi was standing there, Magnolia on her hip. They both looked clean and bright and perfect.

Thomas tried to say something, but he realized it only came out garbled when Vi frowned and inched closer.

"I'm awake," he finally managed to say firmly. "Just a

little groggy." He looked at his arm, all bandaged up. Desk duty for him for a while. *Ugh.*

Then he looked at Vi, and thought, well, maybe he'd just take some medical leave and soak her up.

If she even wants to be there.

"I wasn't sure if I should bring her," Vi said, her voice a little shaky. "I thought the hospital stuff might freak her out, but the hardest part has been keeping her from climbing into bed with you."

"Tata!"

If he wasn't so out of it, he might have cried. He tried to reach his arm out for Magnolia, but it didn't quite work that way yet. "Heya, sweets. You're both a sight for sore eyes."

Vi smiled at that, but her eyes were full of tears. She cleared her throat and looked around, then tugged a chair over to his bedside. She sat, putting Mags in her lap and letting her lean forward and slap at the side of the hospital bed.

"I'm glad you're here."

She reached out, touched his temple. "You saved me."

"You did a lot of saving yourself, Vi."

She nodded, blinking back those tears in her eyes. "I did. I'm proud of myself for that."

"You should be. I am."

She sniffled a little, one tear falling over. "I'm sorry you got hurt. I—"

"I thought we weren't doing sorrys."

She heaved out a sigh. "We're both going to really suck at that."

"So hard."

She laughed, and the sound was a balm for everything. Just everything. She was alive, okay, here. Mags was here. Everything… It would just be all right now. Before his surgery he'd been running on pent-up anger and terror, but now he was just…relieved. Just relieved.

So he watched her as she sat there and let Magnolia play with the hospital bed, and he tried to let that relief really sink in. But it had been so close. And she'd been so brave. And if they hadn't…

She gave a watery laugh. "Stop *looking* at me like that."

"Like what?"

"Like you can't believe I'm alive."

"It's not that, Vi. I just keep thinking, if Franny hadn't called me, I wouldn't have known. For hours more. I was going to be late and…" It was no good. Thinking in what-ifs. He'd told a hundred people that in his line of work before, but it was hard sometimes. Hard to let go of how close a call they'd had. "I was going to be late. I was going to buy a ring."

"A ring?"

"An *engagement* ring."

"For me?"

He closed his eyes. He wanted to laugh but couldn't quite manage it. "Vi."

"Sorry, I just… Thomas…"

"Don't worry. I'm not going to ask you *now*." He was too tired to open his eyes. Too tired to…

"Why not?"

He blinked them open. She was frowning at him now. Blue eyes…petulant.

"Because… Because we've just been through something traumatic."

"Sure, but you were going to ask me before that." She waved it all away like it didn't matter. And he realized it did and it didn't. It mattered in that it happened, but it didn't *matter* to who they were or what they would be.

"And I would have said yes."

"You would have?"

It was her turn to say only his name in a kind of disapproving tone. "Maybe I wouldn't have been *quite* as sure as I am right now. Maybe there would have been a few doubts about...myself. Not you. Never you. *Myself.* But I don't have them anymore. I saw..." She swallowed against the emotion in her throat. "It's awful, but I watched that woman fall victim to the same thing I did. I saw it, and nothing has ever made me realize how little was my fault than seeing it on someone else." Vi shook her head. "Good thing I've got a therapist, I guess."

He wanted to reach out and touch her but couldn't manage it. So he figured he might as well ask. "Give me your hand, Vi."

She heaved out a sigh, but reached out and took his right hand in hers. She squeezed. Mags babbled.

"Did they tell you what's going on with Dianne and Eric?"

She nodded. "Last I heard, Eric was still alive, but they weren't sure how long he'd last. If he does survive, if he goes to trial, I'm going to testify. Whatever I need to do to put him behind bars, I'm going to."

"Me too, and that's a promise."

She looked down at their joined hands. "Dianne didn't deserve to die."

He wished he had the empathy to agree with her. "She kidnapped you. She might have been his victim, but she made choices that you never made. To hurt other people. You aren't the same."

"Maybe not. But she didn't deserve to die at his hands."

"No, maybe not."

Vi swallowed and shook her head before meeting his

gaze again. "I don't want to celebrate the end of people's lives, but I feel... Free. For the first time in a long time, there aren't any clouds hanging over me."

"So, marry me, Vi. Be my wife. I'll adopt Mags. We'll get her under your name where she belongs. We'll be a family."

Vi nodded. "Yes. I'll marry you." She leaned in carefully, keeping Magnolia from grabbing any wires. "Because we *are* a family."

THEY DIDN'T WAIT to get married. What was the point? Neither of them wanted anything fancy. Just their friends, their family and each other.

But Vi *did* buy Magnolia a ridiculously frilly flower girl dress. And they had to wait a few weeks still, to get their parents out to Bent. Her mother couldn't—wouldn't—make it, but Dad and Suze did. Vi was more at peace with that than she'd ever been.

Thomas could get around and do most things for himself, though he pushed harder than he should. To take care of Mags, to help with whatever wedding things.

And still, she appreciated the time. Where he didn't have to work, and they could sort out how this all would *go*. It wasn't as if they agreed on everything, but merging their lives felt more natural than anything she'd ever done.

Because this year had given her perspective she'd desperately needed. To stop and be grateful for every good thing.

And she had so much good.

On the day of the wedding, she got ready in her old bedroom at the Young Ranch. She was wearing a simple white dress, and she didn't need a lot of fussing to get into it, but still, Audra, Rosalie, Franny and her stepmother all packed into the bedroom and helped her get ready, passing Mags around.

"He was such a skinny thing," Suze kept saying, as if she couldn't quite believe that fifteen years later Thomas might have grown up. "I just can't get over it."

Vi smiled every time. Because sometimes she still saw a glimpse of that skinny teenager in the amazing man he'd become. And she loved them both. Always would.

Once she was ready, they headed outside.

Audra and Rosalie had set up a simple archway, some chairs and a runner down the middle of the chairs to create an aisle. For the past few days, Vi had taken Mags out to do a couple trial runs. Her daughter liked playing with the flower petals more than anything, but Vi knew she wouldn't do that at the wedding.

The chairs were full now with her family and his. And *their* friends. Because the world Thomas had built for himself had folded her and Mags into it. Everyone but Magnolia and her father took their seats as Vi got ready to walk down the aisle.

Thomas stood under the pretty floral arch, waiting for her. Wearing a suit. A big grin on his face.

Vi crouched to Magnolia. "Okay, Mags, do you remember what to do?"

"Tata!"

Vi laughed. "Yep. Throw your flowers and walk down to Tata. Slowly."

She let Magnolia go, and just as Vi had suspected, Mags did not walk slowly or throw flower petals as they'd practiced over and over. She just ran for it. Right to Thomas. Who scooped her up into his arms.

He only winced a little.

Then her father walked her down the aisle. "I always liked Thomas," he whispered.

Vi laughed in spite of herself. "No, you didn't."

"Well, I didn't hate him," he grumbled. And he led her right to Thomas under the arch.

"Hi," he said, and she thought about that moment outside the general store all those months ago. When she'd been at her wits' end, a completely different person.

And all she'd really needed was this man in her life again. Now here he was. Hers. Forever.

"Hi," she offered.

Then they turned to the minister, who gave a short introduction and led them through their vows to become man and wife.

It would take some time to get through the red tape, but by the end of the year, they'd all be Harts.

But it didn't really matter. Not names or paperwork. They were each other's, no matter what. A family.

And that was what she told him, promised him in their vows. While he held her little girl. *Their* little girl.

Because *this* was the life she deserved. And she'd fought for it. Always would. For him, for Mags, for herself.

Always.

* * * * *